THE MAGICAL

Every
TRICK
in the
BOOK

LIZ HEDGECOCK

WHITE
RHINO
BOOKS

For Stephen,
bookworm and proud

'It's nothing personal, Jemma.'

Jemma sat clutching the edge of the chair, taking it very personally.

'I can't say this enough,' said Phoebe, her boss. 'It isn't about the person, it's about the job. And unfortunately, your job is no longer required.'

'That's exactly it,' said Wendy from HR. 'It's a business decision.' Her expression softened a little. 'I know that doesn't make it any easier for you.'

Jemma suspected that she was meant to speak at this point, but she couldn't. All her words had hardened into a tight lump in her throat, and she had a feeling that if she tried to talk, something entirely inappropriate would come out. Not that it mattered now, really.

'Now, of course we have a redundancy package,' said Wendy, and Jemma winced. Wendy had explained her presence at the beginning of the meeting, but Jemma had been so shocked that she had barely taken a word in. The R-word made it final.

That morning she had at last finished the report she'd been working on for most of the week, sent it to her boss, then popped out to Pret for her Friday treat: a chicken and avocado sandwich, a slice of carrot cake, and a flat white. Then she re-entered the open-plan office, and all talk ceased.

'Phoebe asked me to let you know that she'd like to see you,' said Yvonne, Phoebe's PA.

'Oh. OK.' Jemma changed course and began to walk towards Phoebe's office.

'She's up in Meeting Room Four,' said Yvonne.

Jemma's skin prickled. Yvonne was looking at her in a sympathetic sort of way. 'Is it about the report? I didn't think she'd have had time to read it yet—'

'She didn't say what it was about,' said Yvonne, though her expression indicated that she knew.

Jemma walked to her desk, put her lunch down, then took the lift to the meeting-room floor. When she saw Yvonne's expression repeated on her boss's face, *she* knew. Wendy's presence was the icing on the cake. Although suddenly she seemed to have lost her appetite.

Wendy was still talking, and Jemma hastily tuned back in. 'Now, we've decided to let the two years you spent in our graduate scheme count towards your service. That makes four years' service, so we have calculated your redundancy payment as *this*.' She pushed a printout across the glass-topped table. There were various numbers on it, all doing a little dance. Jemma nodded, numb, and pushed the piece of paper towards Wendy.

'Normally you would have a notice period of one month. However, given that we have sprung this on you rather, we shall put you on gardening leave for that month to enable you to look for alternative employment.' She smiled. 'Which I'm sure won't be long in coming.'

'No,' said Phoebe. 'I shall give you an excellent reference. Your conscientiousness and your diligence have been an asset to the company. I am truly sorry to lose you.'

Jemma's thoughts were a blur. No more early mornings in the office with an espresso, saying hello to the others as they came in. No more quick drinks after work with Em, which often turned into staying for happy hour, then going for a pizza, then finding herself tumbling into bed happily drunk at a ridiculously early hour. And no time to organise a leaving do.

'So if I could have your badge, and your door pass?' Wendy held her hand out expectantly. 'Oh, and if any of your files aren't saved on the network drive, could you move those over.'

Jemma bent her head and removed her lanyard. 'The door pass is behind the badge,' she said.

Wendy slid it out to check. 'Excellent,' she said brightly, and ticked two boxes on the sheet of paper in front of her. 'Now, I think we've covered everything. Would you mind signing here to confirm?' She pushed the sheet of paper across the desk to Jemma, with a pen.

Jemma signed the paper without reading it. Odd that her signature was just the same as usual. The same neat loops, the same flourish at the end which she had added when she was fourteen, and kept ever since. What now? She looked at her boss for a cue.

'Would you like me to take you back to the office, Jemma?' Phoebe asked, still with that same sympathetic expression on her face. 'I'm sure you'll want to say goodbye to everyone.'

No, I don't, thought Jemma. 'I'll be OK,' she said, with a brave smile.

When Jemma returned to the main office, every head was down. 'Hi,' she said, wondering if she had become invisible.

There were a few mutters of 'Hi' in response, but all heads remained resolutely bent. Em would have said hi, would have smiled; but Em was on leave today, celebrating her boyfriend's new job.

Jemma felt like shouting at them, asking 'Why did none of you warn me? You obviously all knew.' But that would be mean, and she wasn't a mean person. Just ambitious.

The company's clean-desk policy meant Jemma had little to pack up. A pen pot, a business-card holder, a small fake cactus. It all fitted, along with her lunch, in a canvas tote bag emblazoned with the company name. The irony of becoming a walking advertisement for the company just now wasn't lost on her.

'Bye, everyone,' she said as she opened the door. She didn't bother waiting for a reply.

She had to ask Dawn on reception to buzz her out. 'It's my last day,' she said, as explanation.

'You kept that quiet,' said Dawn, as Jemma wrote her

leaving time in the book. 'Off to bigger and better things?'

'Yes,' said Jemma, and smiled.

***

The city bustled past her as she stood outside the building. *I don't want to go home yet*, she thought. *If I go home, I'll probably sit in front of the TV and cry.* Besides, the thought of packing into a tube, a sardine like any other, repelled her. *I have to do something*, she thought, and started walking. She wasn't entirely sure which direction she was heading in; but she was going west.

Jemma walked past office blocks, and shops, and churches. Gradually the City of London became less and less citified, and she found herself in Covent Garden. But today she wasn't in the mood for boutiques or quirky little speciality shops, so she carried on to Charing Cross Road. Here everything seemed slower. People flicked through boxes of books on the pavement, or pointed at window displays. People didn't hurry; they sauntered, or just stood. So far on her journey Jemma had felt like a slow person in a fast world. Here, it was the other way round. She wandered down the street, ready to stop for anything that took her fancy. But the people loitering in front of shops and in doorways made it hard to see, and she moved on.

Then she noticed a little shop set back from the rest, like a shy person at a party. She looked up at the sign. *Burns Books*, it said, in faded gold on navy. *Secondhand Booksellers.*

'Burns Books?' Jemma said, and laughed. 'What a silly name for a bookshop!' In the window were a box set of *The Lord of the Rings,* a dusty collection of Dickens, and a row of Poldark novels, labelled *Two missing*. It wasn't so much a display as an apology. Jemma opened the door, and went in.

A bell above her head jangled, and a man reading *2000 AD* jumped and hastily put it down on the counter. 'Hello,' he said, frowning. 'What do you want? You're not from the council, are you?' He pushed a hand through his sandy hair.

'No,' said Jemma. 'Would it matter if I was?'

'Sometimes they try and sneak in undercover,' said the man. 'It's to do with business rates.' His eyes narrowed. 'Don't tell me you're from the retail association.'

'Still a no,' said Jemma. 'I just wanted to come in and look at books.' She took a step towards the shelves, but the man unfolded himself from behind the counter and intercepted her.

'Why are you dressed like that, then?' he asked, eyeing her suit and heels.

Jemma eyed him back. 'I could ask you the same question.' He was wearing blue and green tartan trousers, a thick bottle-green velvet waistcoat incredibly unsuitable for the weather, a dress shirt with a pleated front, and a gold lamé bow tie.

'I'll dress how I like, thank you very much,' the man replied, with dignity. 'Which books do you wish to look at?' He said this as if expecting her to back down and admit defeat.

'Novels,' declared Jemma, nose in the air. 'I like novels.'

'The fiction section starts there,' he said, jerking a

thumb at it, and retreated behind the counter.

Jemma approached the shelves, trying to remember the last book she'd read. She liked reading – loved reading, in fact – but somehow those evenings working late or getting merry with Em, and the weekends doing a little bit of extra work to stay ahead, really cut into her reading time.

She scanned the shelves for something impressive. Something which would show this snooty bookseller that she wasn't an illiterate fool who had stumbled into a bookshop by accident. Tolstoy. That should do it.

Her hand stretched towards *Anna Karenina* on the bottom shelf, but before she could grasp it the book was obscured by a blur of marmalade fur. Yellow eyes glared at her. The cat sat down right in front of the book, then without ceremony began to clean its bottom.

'Um, excuse me?' Jemma called.

There was no response, and she had to call again.

'Yes?' the man enquired.

'There's a cat in the way of a book I want to buy.'

'Oh yes, that will be Folio.' And the man returned to his comic.

'I don't think you understand,' said Jemma. 'I need you to move the cat.'

The man stared at her over the top of his comic. 'I don't think Folio would like that.'

'He's a cat,' said Jemma. 'I'm a customer. Or at least, I'd like to be a customer, but I'm finding it difficult.'

'I know!' the man cried, looking as pleased as if he had made an important discovery. 'I can make a note of the book you want, and your name. When Folio moves, I'll put the book in a safe place and you can come back for it!'

Jemma stared at him. 'Or I could go to another bookshop.'

An unpleasant shiver ran down her spine. Really, the bookshop was remarkably cold. And it smelt a bit damp. She straightened up, and looked around her. *It's like going back in time.* The counter was dark wood, probably mahogany, and on it stood a huge brass cash register. The shelves were sagging pine, and the floor was wood in a herringbone pattern, like in an old-fashioned school. There were no posters, no promotional materials, no recommendations… The only attractive thing in the bookshop was a red leather button-back armchair with a tapestry cushion. That looked warm and inviting. She took a step towards it, and the cat – Folio, was it? – dashed past her, leapt into the armchair, and settled himself down. *What a miserable dump.*

Jemma bent, retrieved the book, and took it to the counter. 'I'd like this, please,' she said.

The man inspected it, and shrugged. 'Never read it myself.' He opened the front cover. 'Two pounds fifty, please.'

Jemma held out her phone, and the man looked at it. 'That's worth more than two pounds fifty,' he said.

Jemma put it back in her bag and took a card from her purse. The man shook his head again.

'Good grief,' said Jemma, staring. 'You actually want money?'

'That's how it works,' said the man. He pushed buttons on the cash register and with a great clanking and ringing, figures pinged up in the top window.

Jemma opened her purse and handed over a two-pound coin and a fifty-pence piece. 'I'm afraid I'm fresh out of shillings,' she said.

'Very funny,' said the man. 'I can write you a receipt, if you wish.'

'Don't worry about it,' said Jemma.

'Would you like a bag, then?' He indicated a nail driven into the shelf behind him, from which hung plain brown-paper bags on a string.

'I'll put it in my own bag, thanks,' said Jemma. She felt something pushing at her ankles. It was the cat, Folio. 'Oh, he likes me,' she said, bending to stroke the cat.

'I wouldn't do that,' said the man. 'He isn't very friendly.'

Folio looked up at her, then put his head against her leg and butted. Jemma took a step back, and he advanced and butted her again. *He's trying to push me out of the shop*, she thought. *Well, that's fine by me. I don't think I'll be returning here in a hurry.* 'Bye,' she said, and walked briskly towards the door.

As she reached for the handle Jemma noticed a small white card stuck into the wood with a drawing pin. *Help Wanted*, it said, in elegant copperplate script. *It certainly is*, thought Jemma, with a smile. *I don't think I've ever seen such a sorry excuse for a bookshop in my whole life.* And with that comforting thought, she closed the door firmly behind her.

Jemma felt unaccountably nervous as she walked down Charing Cross Road on Monday morning. *It's only a bookshop*, she told herself. *I could work anywhere I like.*

She had spent the weekend trying to decide what she wanted to do with the rest of her life. She had made lists. She had read articles about how self-made millionaires under thirty got their start. She had updated her CV. But still, when she closed her eyes, the scruffy bookshop with so much potential kept reappearing. *I could make something of that*, she thought. *I really could.*

She hadn't said anything to Em when she rang on Saturday afternoon. 'How are you, Jemma,' Em had enquired, with a wheelbarrow-full of concern in her voice. 'I'm sorry I couldn't be there yesterday. I'd have rung earlier, but I've just got up. Damon had tickets for the races, you see, as a leaving present from the agency, and then there was a boat trip, and it got a bit messy—'

'You knew, then,' said Jemma, feeling like a flat glass of lemonade.

'I didn't exactly know,' said Em. 'I mean, I'd heard talk. But you know I don't spread rumours.'

Em had been in the same intake of the graduate scheme as Jemma. Despite cheerfully admitting that she didn't know one end of a spreadsheet from the other, she had risen in the company through what she called a series of happy accidents. If Jemma hadn't been her friend, she would have envied Em tremendously. She had shiny dark hair that never seemed to need washing or cutting, and looked good in whatever she wore.

'I'm going to regard it as an opportunity,' said Jemma. 'A chance to do something different. The company wasn't right for me; that was the problem. Our values weren't aligned.'

'That's exactly what I think,' said Em. 'Do you fancy going for a quick drink?'

Jemma wrinkled her nose at her pyjama bottoms and T-shirt, and examined the split ends in her reddish-brown hair. 'Maybe not today,' she said. 'I'm taking some downtime to consider my new direction.' Plus she didn't feel ready to face Damon, whom she found hard going at the best of times. With a new job, he'd be insufferable.

'Oh, OK,' said Em. 'Well, Damon and I will be in the Grapes if you change your mind. I expect we'll be there for some time.'

And so, after considerable research, Jemma found herself striding down Charing Cross Road wearing ballerina flats, wide-legged black trousers, a smart-casual top, and her second-best work jacket, ready to make an impression.

The shop was closed.

Jemma looked at her watch, and tutted. The door had a brass knocker in the shape of a mythical creature; she wasn't sure quite what. Jemma lifted it, and brought it down sharply three times.

After two minutes, she knocked again. This time she was greeted with a yowl. Then she heard a muttered word which sounded rude, and someone fumbling with the lock.

The man who had been in the shop on Friday opened the door. He was wearing a mustard-coloured dressing gown over sky-blue silk pyjamas. 'Not today, thank you,' he said sharply.

Jemma put a foot in the door. 'I'm here to help,' she said.

'What, at this time of the morning?' The man looked incredulous. 'I don't need my soul saving, thank you very much.'

'I meant in the bookshop,' said Jemma. 'Help wanted?'

The man stared at her. 'I never expected anyone to answer,' he said. Then, grudgingly, 'I suppose you'd better come in.' He opened the door wider. 'Here, take a seat.' He indicated the armchair. 'I'll go and, um, get dressed.'

Jemma did as she was told and gazed around the shop. It was as dilapidated as she remembered. *Good. That means I can make more of a difference.* She opened her large work handbag, took out a folder, and put it on her knee, ready. At least that cat didn't seem to be around.

'Sorry about that,' said the man's voice. He reappeared, now dressed in a navy velvet suit with a crisp white shirt and a floppy black bow at his neck. Jemma wondered how on earth he had managed to get changed in such a short time. 'So.' He stood in front of Jemma, hands clasped, rocking gently on the balls of his feet.

'Aren't you going to interview me?' asked Jemma.

'Oh,' said the man. 'Um, yes, I suppose I am.'

'I'm Jemma James,' said Jemma, standing up and extending a hand. She had to look up quite a long way, as the man was at least a foot taller than she was.

He shook her hand firmly. 'Raphael Burns, owner and proprietor of Burns Books. Pleased to meet you.' He nodded, and Jemma sat down.

'About that,' she said. 'Do you really think Burns Books is a good name for a bookshop?'

The man seemed rather offended. 'The shop has been called Burns Books ever since it opened,' he said. 'It's been in the family for a long time.'

Jemma took that as a no. 'Would you like to see my qualifications?' she said, opening her folder. 'I've brought my GCSE, A-level and degree certificates, and my management diploma.' She held out a sheaf of papers, which the man took and paged through – possibly, she suspected, more from good manners than anything else.

'All most satisfactory,' he said, handing them back. 'When can you start?'

'Aren't you going to ask me any questions?' said Jemma. 'My previous experience, or why I want the job, or what I could bring to it?' Then she reflected that her lack of retail experience might count against her. 'Actually,' she said, 'I've put together a short-term action plan. Would you like me to present it to you?'

Raphael shuddered. 'Would you like a cup of tea?' he said.

'Yes please,' said Jemma. *While he's gone*, she thought, *I'll get my bullet points in order.*

She was fully prepared when Raphael Burns returned, bearing a tray with a cloth, two china cups and saucers, and a large teapot with a Space Invaders tea cosy over the top. 'I thought of some questions while the tea was brewing,' he said.

'Oh good,' said Jemma, composing herself. She hoped that his previous absentmindedness hadn't been an act, and he wasn't about to skewer her with something she hadn't thought of.

Raphael put the tray on the counter, poured out, and delivered a cup of tea with milk and one sugar, as Jemma had requested. Then he brought the chair from behind the counter, placed it facing her, and sat down. It was slightly too small for him, and he inhabited it like a wooden artist's figure arranged to show discomfort. 'This is my first question,' he said grandly. 'Do you like cats?'

As if on cue, Folio sauntered into the room, meowed at Jemma, then jumped into her lap, sitting on her papers and kneading them with his paws.

'Um, yes,' she said. 'Yes, I do like cats.'

Folio looked round at her and his golden eyes narrowed. The sound of tearing paper grew slightly louder.

'Excellent!' exclaimed Raphael. 'Now for my second

question. Do you mind being bored?'

'Did you say bored?' asked Jemma, wondering if this was a trap.

'Yes, I did. Do you mind being bored, sometimes for hours at a time?'

'I don't think that question applies to me, really,' said Jemma. 'I find I'm hardly ever bored, as I can always think of something to do. For example, if business was slow in the shop, I could spend time writing and scheduling posts on the shop's social media feeds.'

'But we don't have any social media feeds,' said Raphael.

'I know,' said Jemma, triumphantly. 'I checked. And that, if I may say so, is one of your problems. Social media would give you additional shop windows onto the world. With the right targeted content, you could bring people here from far and wide.'

Raphael picked up his cup and drained it. He was clearly impressed.

'Another thing I could do during downtime in the shop,' said Jemma, 'would be to create eye-catching themed displays of books which we have in the shop. For example, you have *The Lord of the Rings* in the window, and I'm sure you must have Harry Potter books knocking around. We could make a display with a starry backcloth, and pointy hats, and maybe a flying broomstick or two.'

'Good heavens,' said Raphael.

'And I'm sure I could organise a way for the shop to take credit and debit cards,' said Jemma. 'You know, bring you into the twenty-first century.'

15

'I'm really not sure that's necessary,' said Raphael. He looked down his nose at her. 'All right, I shall employ you.'

'Wait a minute,' said Jemma. 'Aren't you going to ask me if I have any questions?'

'Do I have to?' asked Raphael.

'Yes, you do,' said Jemma, who had been on a recruitment course. She tried to remember what she had written, since Folio showed no sign of moving. 'What is the salary?'

Raphael looked nonplussed, then rather cunning. 'What did you earn in your previous job?'

Jemma wondered whether her answer would give him a heart attack, then decided to be truthful. Perhaps he was an eccentric millionaire who kept the shop as a hobby.

From Raphael's reaction, he was not an eccentric millionaire. He goggled at her. 'What on earth are you doing here, then?'

Jemma was prepared for this. 'I decided it was time for a change of focus,' she said grandly. 'I enjoyed my previous job, but it was taking up too much of my life. I want to shift down a gear and engage in a role I can give my heart to.' She remembered all the nights she had worked late, polishing reports for Phoebe, and crossed her fingers. 'I would be prepared to take a pay cut' – she named a figure which was approximately half of her previous salary – 'with the understanding that I would be rewarded appropriately for improving the bottom line of the shop.'

'The bottom line?' said Raphael, leaning down to look at the skirting board.

'The profits,' said Jemma, wondering if this man had ever read a business book in his life. Actually, she was pretty confident that he hadn't.

'All right, so that's salary,' said Raphael. 'What other questions do you have?'

'How many weeks' holiday will I have per year?' asked Jemma. 'What will my working hours be? Do you open on Sundays? Do you ever open in the evenings?'

Raphael held up his hands to ward her off. 'The shop hours are nine till five, Monday to Friday,' he said.

Jemma couldn't believe her ears. 'Not Saturdays? Not the busiest shopping day?'

'Not Saturdays,' Raphael said firmly.

Jemma shrugged. 'Fair enough. What about holidays?'

The cunning look came over his face again. 'What did you get in your previous job?'

Jemma told him.

'The same, then,' he said.

Jemma gave him a mental tick. 'Do you have a benefits package? Discounts, pension scheme, luncheon vouchers?'

'I could give you ten per cent off the books,' said Raphael. 'But to be honest, you can read those for free when it's quiet. Which it generally is. And I expect I'll buy you a coffee occasionally.'

Jemma sighed. 'That'll do,' she said. In any case, when more branches of Burns Books opened, she would be able to pay into her pension.

Raphael waited. 'Do you have any more questions?' he asked, as if opening the door to a tiger's cage.

Jemma considered, then decided she had probably put

him through enough. 'Not just now,' she said.

'Well, in that case,' said Raphael, 'I suppose you can start.' He extended a hand carefully over Folio, and Jemma shook it again. 'I'll go and find you an apron.' He eyed her. 'It might be a bit big for you. The previous assistant was taller.'

'Oh, that's a question I should ask,' said Jemma. 'Why did the previous assistant leave?'

Raphael looked extremely uncomfortable. 'He found that the post didn't agree with him.' His eye fell on Folio.

'Oh,' said Jemma, 'was he allergic to cats?'

'Yes,' said Raphael. 'Or something like that. It was more that Folio was allergic to him. He was a nice chap, too. But not everyone is suited to a bookshop.' He regarded Jemma thoughtfully. 'In fact, I think we should begin with a week's trial. To see how you get on with the shop, and how the shop gets on with you.'

'That's a good idea,' said Jemma. *After all*, she thought, *if it's as boring as he says, a week might be plenty.* 'So, until Friday?'

Raphael looked as if he were solving a complicated sum in his head. 'Yes,' he declared, eventually. 'Until Friday. I'll go and find that apron.' He uncurled himself from the chair and disappeared into the back room.

Jemma gazed down at Folio, who had fallen asleep in her lap, bits of paper caught between his claws. *I'm in*, she thought. *I've done it. I've landed a new job. And if I have anything to do with it, there will be changes around here.*

Folio purred in his sleep, stretched out a lazy paw, and sank his claws into her thigh.

Chapter 3

'Do I have to wear that?' asked Jemma, eyeing the brown apron which Raphael was holding up. It would probably cover her from neck to ankles, not to mention twice round.

'Well no, you don't have to,' said Raphael. 'But you might get a bit dusty otherwise.'

'Clothes are washable,' said Jemma. 'I mean, you don't see the assistants in Waterstones wearing—'

'Perhaps I should take this opportunity to mention,' said Raphael, 'that we'd rather you didn't talk about…' He lowered his voice. '*Other bookshops*.'

Jemma stared at him. 'Why ever not? They're our competitors.'

'Yes, yes, competitors is fine,' said Raphael. 'Rivals, also good. But don't name names.'

He probably finds it embarrassing, thought Jemma. 'Is it a sensitive point?' she asked, with a sympathetic smile.

Then she wondered if her sympathetic smile looked the same as Phoebe's, and put it away.

'It is,' said Raphael. 'Thank you for understanding.'

'That's quite all right,' said Jemma. 'But I'd rather not wear the apron, if you don't mind.'

The letterbox rattled. 'Aha, the post!' cried Raphael, and dived for the doormat. He gathered up five or six envelopes and leafed through them. 'Bill . . . bill . . . junk mail . . . bill…' Jemma noticed that several of the envelopes had red ink on them. He opened a plain white envelope, unfolded the sheet within, scowled at it, then crumpled it into a ball and stuffed it in his pocket. 'And that was the post,' he said, going behind the counter, opening a drawer, and dropping the rest of the envelopes in unopened. 'Now the day can begin.'

'Shouldn't you open the bills?' Jemma wondered when, or if, she would be paid.

'Don't worry,' said Raphael. 'I have a special time put aside for dealing with things like that.'

'Oh, good,' said Jemma, pleased to learn there was some sort of organisation to this enterprise. 'When is that?'

'When the man arrives to cut it off, usually,' said Raphael. 'No sense in dealing with these things before you have to.'

Jemma opened her mouth to argue, then thought better of it. This felt like a battle for another time. Besides, she was curious to learn how the bookshop worked. If it did.

'When opening up,' said Raphael, 'the first job is to unlock the door. Which we've already done today, so we're ahead of ourselves.' He looked rather impressed with himself. 'Then, we turn the sign around.' He demonstrated. 'Next, we raise the blind in the shop window, like so.' He moved to the window, tugged on the cord, and the blind shot up. 'Voilà. Finally, we switch on the lights. One at a time, please. You never know.' He moved to a brass panel of toggle switches by the door, tensed himself, and pushed one down.

A dim light flickered on.

Raphael exhaled. 'And so on.' Gradually the shop became slightly brighter than it had been before. 'Do you need to make any notes?'

'I think I've got it so far,' said Jemma.

'Next, we check the till. You press this button to open it.' The drawer shot out with a ping. 'Now, I usually write down how much is in the till at the end of each day, so that we know where we're at. If it's a bit empty in the morning, there are some bank bags of change in this drawer.' He opened it, then closed it again. 'But I think we'll do.'

'So you don't cash up properly at the end of each day?' asked Jemma.

Raphael looked blank. 'Do you think I should?'

'Aren't you bothered about getting burgled?'

Raphael stared at her, then his face crumpled into a laugh. 'Burgled? Us? I don't think that's likely. We have good security, and Folio is an excellent guard cat.'

'I'm sure he is,' said Jemma, studying Folio, who was washing himself in the middle of the Science section.

'As a rule of thumb,' said Raphael, 'I tend to visit the bank when the till money gets above fifty pounds. That's a nice round number.'

Jemma's eyebrows shot into her fringe. She wanted to say many things at this point, but settled for 'I see.'

'Now, working the till,' said Raphael. 'When a customer buys a book, you check the price, then press the appropriate buttons so that the right amount comes up in the little window at the top. Then you press the *Sale* button, and the drawer opens. I'll show you properly if we get a customer.'

'What if they buy, say, two books?' asked Jemma. 'Do you add the number up first, then put it in? Or do you put the two numbers in separately?'

Raphael's brow furrowed. 'I don't think we'll worry about that just yet,' he said. 'That's all you need to know.'

'But what about dealing with customers?'

The blank look came over Raphael's face again. 'Um, I say hello to them, and then I generally let them get on with it. Obviously, if they ask me a direct question I answer them. After all, I wouldn't wish to be rude—'

The shop bell jangled.

'I'll watch and learn, shall I?' said Jemma, and took a step back. She unbuttoned her jacket and hung it on the old-fashioned coat stand next to the counter, ready for action.

'Good morning,' Raphael said politely to the somewhat frazzled woman who entered the shop.

'Good morning,' she said, looking about her. 'I wonder if you could help me. My sister is in hospital, and her TV doesn't work, and she's bored out of her brain.'

'Oh,' said Raphael. 'I'm afraid I'm not good with

machinery. Especially not when electricity is involved.'

Jemma took a decisive step forward. 'What does she like to read?'

'Well, I took her my daughter's copy of *Jane Eyre*, and she was enjoying that, but I had to get it back because my daughter has to write an essay on it by Thursday.'

'Right, *Jane Eyre*. Charlotte Brontë.' Jemma went to General Fiction and found the Bs. 'We have two copies of that, and one copy of *Villette* by the same author. Oh, and one copy each of *Agnes Grey* and *The Tenant of Wildfell Hall*.' She thought. 'Would she like Jane Austen, do you think?'

The woman laughed. 'I know she liked *Pride and Prejudice* when it was on TV. Especially the bit where Mr Darcy dived into the lake.'

Jemma moved along to the As. 'We've got three of those and two copies of *Emma*. Oh, and a *Mansfield Park*.' She put her chin on the pile to keep it stable, took them to the counter, and spread them out.

The woman looked at the books. 'That's a lot,' she said.

'Of course you don't have to take them all,' said Jemma, 'but I could probably do you a deal if you buy a few.' She glanced across at Raphael, who was watching the transaction rather as one would watch a cobra emerging from a snake charmer's basket. 'I take it we can do a deal?'

'Yes,' said Raphael, as if hypnotised. 'We can do a deal.'

The woman brightened. 'Oh well, in that case…' Her hand hovered over the books. 'That one . . . and those two . . . and that one. And that *Pride and Prejudice*.' Her finger landed decisively on Colin Firth's chest.

'So that's five books.' Jemma checked the prices. 'At two pounds fifty each…' She glanced at Raphael. 'Can we do ten pounds? That's one book free.'

Raphael jumped. 'I'm sorry, what did you say?'

'Ten pounds for these five books,' Jemma said patiently. 'That's fair, isn't it?'

'I'll take them,' said the woman, digging out her purse. 'And I have a ten-pound note, which is lucky.'

'Isn't it,' said Jemma. She moved behind the counter and pushed the *10* button on the cash register, then the *00* button. The numbers appeared in the window. 'What do I do now?' she muttered to Raphael.

'Press the *Sale* button,' said Raphael, pointing.

'Oh yes, that's it,' said Jemma. 'Sorry, it's my first day.'

'Are you enjoying it?' asked the woman, handing over the note.

'Yes,' said Jemma. 'I am. Oh, and if you need any more books for your sister, you know where we are.'

'Indeed I do,' the woman replied. 'It's funny, but I hadn't noticed the shop before today. I think it's because you're set back.'

'Maybe that's it,' said Jemma, vowing to establish the shop's social media presence at the first opportunity. 'Would you like a bag? Or a receipt?'

'Oh yes, a bag would be good.'

Jemma pulled a paper bag off the string, then wrote *Burns Books* on it, and copied the telephone number from the dial of the black Bakelite phone next to her. 'There,' she said, slipping the paperbacks inside. 'If you want to

24

check if we have a book, you can phone us and ask.'

'What a good idea,' said the woman. 'Must go, I was meant to be at work ten minutes ago.' She picked up the bag and scurried off.

'That was fun,' said Jemma, as the shop door closed behind her. 'Do you have any feedback for me?'

'Er, feedback?' said Raphael.

'Yes, on my handling of the retailer-customer interface,' said Jemma.

Raphael flinched. 'You did very well,' he said. 'In fact, I think you're ready for one of the more advanced aspects of working in a bookshop.'

Jemma could feel herself puffing up with pride. 'What's that?' she asked.

Raphael beamed. 'Now, don't be too disappointed if you don't get it right first time. Most people don't.'

'I'll give it my best shot,' said Jemma. 'What is it?'

Raphael looked very serious. 'Do you think you could possibly make us both a cup of tea?'

Chapter 4

No, Jemma told herself sternly. *You are going to avoid the takeaway, go home, and cook yourself a proper meal.*

But I have to stand up to do that. I've been on my feet all day—

Then you'll have to get used to it. Jemma took a deep breath, looked straight ahead, and marched past the takeaway. Enticing smells of grease and pepperoni assaulted her nostrils. *I am strong. I can do this. Anyway, I had pizza for lunch.*

She had been surprised when Raphael announced that he was nipping out for lunch at twelve thirty, then returned with a pizza box emblazoned with the logo of the takeaway next door, Snacking Cross Road. 'I hope you like anchovies,' he said, lifting the lid and revealing a pizza Napoli.

'Ooh, thanks,' said Jemma. She salivated at the aroma.

Breakfast had been light, as she had been too nervous to eat much, and had happened what seemed like a very long time ago.

Raphael lifted a slice in his long fingers and took a hefty bite. 'Well, go on then,' he said, through the pizza.

Jemma glanced at the door. 'Should I wait?' she asked. 'A customer might come in.'

'And the pizza *will* get cold,' said Raphael, giving her a severe look.

'Fair point,' said Jemma, and dived in.

No, there was definitely no excuse to stop by the takeaway tonight. The shop had closed at five o'clock precisely, and they had cashed up and found £152.50 in the till, which Raphael pronounced a record for a Monday. He locked it in the safe, then glanced at his watch, cried 'Good heavens, it's almost half past!', and shooed her out of the shop.

I'll wear more comfortable shoes tomorrow, she thought as she walked down her road, wincing as her heel rubbed yet again. *Are Converse acceptable?* She decided that if dress suits and gold bow ties were OK, then baseball boots would be fine. Especially since she would be behind the counter a lot of the time.

She arrived at the slightly dilapidated Victorian townhouse where she had a studio flat, let herself in, and wished, not for the first time, that her landlord would put in a lift. *I can probably cancel my gym membership*, she thought. *It isn't as if I went anyway, and the shop will keep me fit.* She climbed up the grand staircase to the third floor. As usual, the slightly wonky B on the door of the flat irked her. *Not much I can do about it*, she thought, and opened the door.

Jemma kicked off her shoes, resisted the call of the sofa, and went to investigate the cupboards in the kitchenette. She found pasta, a tin of tomatoes, a tin of beans, and in the fridge, a heel of cheese and some dried-out ham. She checked in the bread bin, but the three slices of bread left had green speckles blooming on them, and she put them in the bin. 'Pasta it is,' she said, and filled a pan with water.

Even after filling a bowl with the resultant cheese and tomato gloop, there was still plenty left. *I can have it again tomorrow*, she thought. She flopped on the sofa, switched on the TV, and was puzzled for a moment when she didn't see what she expected. *Of course, it's still early*, she thought, channel-surfing until she found something suitable to accompany forking pasta into her face.

She had just put a particularly cheesy, tomatoey forkful into her mouth when her mobile rang. 'Mmff,' she said, reached for her phone, and looked at the display.

Em.

Jemma pressed *Accept*. 'Hi, Em,' she said, after swallowing.

'I called to see how you were doing,' said Em. 'I hope you're all right.'

Jemma smiled to herself. 'I'm fine, thanks. I haven't long got in from work. I've been cooking.'

'Work?' said Em. 'What are you doing?' Suddenly a loud metallic-sounding voice boomed unintelligibly. 'Sorry, just waiting for my train. You did say work, didn't you?'

'Yes, I found a job,' said Jemma, feeling exceptionally perky. 'I'm working in a bookshop.'

'Oh,' said Em. 'That's a bit different.' A pause. 'Are you enjoying it?'

'Yes,' said Jemma. 'It's an independent one, on Charing Cross Road.'

'Oh, right,' said Em. 'Doesn't that have loads of bookshops?'

'That's right,' said Jemma. 'My one is called Burns Books.'

The tannoy boomed out again, and Jemma waited patiently for Em's congratulations. The noise ceased, but Em was still silent. 'Em? Are you still there?'

'Yes, I'm still here.' Em sounded faint, but down in the tube the signal was always poor. 'Was that Burns Books you said? Only—'

'Have you heard of it?' asked Jemma, eagerly. 'It isn't a big shop, but it's got lots of potential. I think I can make a real difference.'

'Um,' said Em. 'It's just that – My train's here, but I read something. I'll send it to you. You haven't signed a contract or anything, have you?'

Jemma laughed. 'Raphael isn't that kind of boss,' she said. 'But what did you—'

'Got to go, bye, bye.'

Jemma looked at the phone for a moment, then put it down and scooped up more pasta. *Maybe she's jealous of my new start*, she thought to herself, chewing.

She had just finished the bowl when her phone pinged

29

with a message. *You might want to read this. Sorry.*

Jemma clicked on the attachment. It was an article: *The Ten Worst Bookshops in Britain.* It was from a website that specialised in listicles, and beneath the title it said, in smaller letters: *Information taken from The Bookseller's Companion and social media.* And at number two – not even the top spot – was Burns Books.

Looking for a satisfying shopping experience? Then don't come here. The owner dresses like a failed Doctor Who who's found a bookshop from the bad old days and brought it kicking and screaming into the present. He couldn't care less about the customers, the shop is a death trap, and if the shop doesn't get you, the cat will. How the shop keeps running is a complete mystery, but I wouldn't advise you to try and solve it by going there.

Jemma's mouth twitched. She had to admit that, as descriptions went, it wasn't entirely inaccurate. She closed the article and hit *Reply. That was an interesting read*, she texted. *Thanks for sending it. The shop does have a lot of potential.*

She yawned widely, and covered her mouth. *I shall read in bed,* she decided, and opened out the sofa-bed. *If I'm going to turn the shop around, I'll need to be well rested.*

***

Folio, now the size of a tiger, roared at Jemma, and she had to build a barricade of books to keep herself safe. She had just put the last book into place when Folio leapt on top of it and books rained down on her. 'No!' she cried, flinging up her hands. Then she blinked, removed *Anna Karenina* from her face, and realised that the roaring was a loud rock number which, in her view, was completely inappropriate for breakfast radio.

She got ready, had a large bowl of cornflakes, and set off for the tube. As before, she had to knock for admission, but at least this time Raphael was dressed. Today's outfit was a tweed suit with elbow patches, a pink shirt, and a navy cravat with stars on. Jemma remembered the article, and tried not to smirk.

'You're early again,' said Raphael, with a yawn. 'Perhaps I should sort you out with a set of keys, and then you can open up when you arrive.'

'Oh, could I?' said Jemma, beaming.

He stared at her, nonplussed. 'If you like,' he said slowly.

A yowl came from behind him. Jemma peeped and saw Folio, now normal-sized, yawning. 'Hello, Folio,' she said, extending a hand.

Folio put his head on one side, considered her hand, then walked off.

'Right, important business,' said Raphael, rubbing his hands. 'Tea!'

'But aren't we going to refill the shelves?' said Jemma. 'We sold quite a few books yesterday. Shouldn't we put more stock out? Where is the stock?'

'In the stockroom,' said Raphael. 'Where else would it be?'

'OK,' said Jemma. 'Do we know what's in there?'

'Broadly, yes,' said Raphael. 'Specifically, not really. I

just open a box when I feel the urge, and see what's inside.'

'Would you mind if I had a look?' asked Jemma.

Raphael shrugged. 'Be my guest. If you go into the back room, it's the door on the right.'

'Do I need a key?'

His only response was a laugh.

Jemma went into the back room and faced the door. What would she find behind it? She imagined a broom-cupboard-like space, with boxes stacked one on top of the other and barely room to turn round. She took a deep breath, and opened the door.

'The light switch is on the left,' called Raphael. 'One at a time, remember.'

Jemma snapped on the light. 'Woah.'

It was like the warehouse at the end of *Raiders of the Lost Ark*. OK, maybe not that big, but *big*.

'How does this room fit into the shop?' Jemma muttered to herself. 'It's like the Tardis. But stop with the Doctor Who comparisons, it's getting weird.' She walked down the middle aisle of the three. Boxes squatted on metal shelves, seven rows high, which reached to the ceiling. She lifted a box out carefully, and saw at least two more behind. As far as she could tell, not one box was labelled. 'How on earth does he find anything?' she said, aloud.

The answer came to her immediately. *He doesn't.*

Jemma's sense of order, of how things ought to be, bristled. *He needs a spreadsheet,* she thought. *A big spreadsheet. No, he doesn't need it. The shop needs it.* She resolved to bring her laptop in the next day and start cataloguing this fearful mess. *Well,* she conceded, *not exactly a mess.* After all, the books were in boxes. It was a mess made to look as if it wasn't a mess, which was even worse.

She took the box she had selected through to the shop, then returned to switch off the light and close the door. She found Raphael regarding the box with curiosity. 'I wonder what's inside,' he said.

'If you labelled the boxes,' said Jemma, 'you'd know.'

'Where's the fun in that?' said Raphael. 'This is like Christmas.'

'Let's hope it's a good Christmas,' said Jemma, grimly. 'Do you have any scissors?'

The lid of the box was taped down. Jemma cut into it carefully, opened the flaps, and revealed a stack of Mills and Boon romances and, sitting next to them, what looked like a complete set of CS Forester's Hornblower novels.

'Strange bedfellows,' she murmured. 'Oh well, I might as well put them out, seeing as the box is open.'

'Pass me one, would you,' said Raphael.

Jemma picked up *Mr Midshipman Hornblower.*

'No, from the other side.'

Jemma shrugged, and passed him *A Debutante in Disguise.*

'I've always wanted to read one of these,' Raphael said, opening it. 'Never got round to it.' He sat in the armchair, took out a pair of reading glasses, and settled them on his long nose. Folio hopped onto his lap, and was peacefully asleep within seconds.

'Guess I'd better restock the shelves, then,' said Jemma, but there was no response.

Jemma put out the books, turned the sign, raised the blind, switched on the lights, and checked the till, but not a customer appeared. In the end she took out her copy of *Anna Karenina* and attempted to read the first chapter. But somehow images of a roaring Folio, a bookshop travelling through space, and an empty till kept getting between her and the pages. She glanced across at Raphael, still reading, and the words of the article echoed in her head. How *does* the bookshop keep running?

Chapter 5

Jemma was no wiser on that subject by Friday. It had been a whirlwind of a week. She had sold, in her estimation, hundreds of books to a range of people, from harried office workers looking for 'something on emotional intelligence' to bewildered and often bedraggled tourists in Harry Potter scarves, who arrived in the shop asking if she could direct them to the Leaky Cauldron.

At first she had told them, rather shortly, that while the Leaky Cauldron was on Charing Cross Road in the books, it was filmed elsewhere in London. Then she wised up, gathered Harry Potter books, and displayed them in the window, along with a straw broom she had found at a hardware shop down the road and a witch's hat from a fancy-dress shop. She had assumed that they would burn through their entire Harry Potter stock in one day. Somehow, though, every time she went to the stockroom, she struck lucky and found yet another box of Harry Potters in her random selection.

'It's a bit odd,' she said to Raphael, one day.

'What's odd?' he asked, looking wary.

'Well, because of the shop display we have lots of people wanting Harry Potter books, and somehow, those are what I'm finding in the stockroom.'

'Mmm,' said Raphael. 'Probably just coincidence.' And sure enough, the next box Jemma opened turned out to contain a mixture of books by Zadie Smith, China Miéville, and Gabriel Garcia Marquez.

But the shop was definitely making more money; of that Jemma was certain. She made sure to always be present at cashing-up time, and on some days they took as much as three hundred pounds. 'I don't know what the bank manager will make of this,' said Raphael.

'They'll probably be very pleased,' said Jemma.

'They'll probably think I'm up to something,' said Raphael.

'I told you that getting the shop on social media was a good idea,' said Jemma. So far the shop had a Facebook page, a Twitter feed, and an Instagram account. She liked the idea of TikTok, but suspected that making videos with Raphael in the shop would be difficult.

She had even attempted to catalogue the books, but that hadn't gone to plan. It ought to have been perfectly straightforward, if laborious. But somehow her laptop kept saving the spreadsheet to weird locations, and when she found and reopened it the data was corrupt, or one of the columns had vanished. In the end she gave it up as a bad job. *There's probably professional software I could get to do this*, she thought. *Maybe l could persuade Raphael that it's an investment.* And she left it at that.

And now it was Friday, and the end of her trial week. Her clock radio woke her with 'Don't Leave Me This Way'. She tried to read that as a positive sign that the shop couldn't cope without her, but didn't even manage to convince herself. She hunkered under the duvet and stared at the ceiling, where a crack was creeping towards the light fitting. *Come on Jemma, best foot forward*, she told herself. But she waited until the Pet Shop Boys' 'Opportunity' was playing before getting up. You never knew.

Ridiculous, she thought, throwing off her duvet. *As if I've ever been superstitious. Superstition gets you nowhere.* But she felt better as she got ready, humming along.

That's probably because you're eating better, she thought. *Although Kris from the takeaway probably thinks I've died.*

On Wednesday, after the previous night's palatial supper of leftover pasta, and realising that if she didn't do something she would be having a bowl of baked beans for tea, she had borrowed a book called *Easy Suppers* from the cookery section and visited Nafisa's Mini-Market two doors down. It had taken her an hour and a half to cook a meal which allegedly took twenty-five minutes, but while it looked nothing like the photograph, it tasted nice. And she couldn't feel her arteries closing up as they did when she wolfed down one of Kris's offerings…

Jemma realised the time, and dashed to the tube station. The first train was already full so she waited for the next, which took ten minutes to come and was full again. By the time she managed to squeeze onto a train then dash to the shop, it was five to nine. 'Sorry I'm late,' she panted, as Raphael opened the door in his usual unhurried manner. 'It was the trains. They were awful, and I had to wait ages.'

'Never mind,' said Raphael, absently. 'You're here now. I was just about to open.'

There was no hint of reproof in either his voice or his face, but Jemma still felt it. *Nice one, Jemma,* she thought to herself as she scurried to the window and pulled up the blind. *Stellar move, being almost late on the day when your boss decides if he's keeping you or not.* She remembered a day, perhaps a year ago, when the tube had let her down, and she had arrived in the office at her actual start time instead of her usual hour earlier. The office had given her a round of applause and raucous cheers, with cries of 'Here she is at last!' and 'We were going to call the police!' Even Phoebe had come out of her office to comment. Jemma had taken it with a smile; but she had never been so late, as she thought of it, again.

The shop was quiet that morning and Jemma kept her head down, getting stock on the shelves (today's boxes held travel guides, books on hobbies, and manuals about budgeting). 'I thought it would be busier on a Friday,' she ventured at eleven o'clock, when their only customer so far, a man looking for books on the Indian railways, had departed with three large hardbacks under his arm.

'It goes in waves,' said Raphael. 'I'd like to tell you that it varies with the weather, or the season, or what's on television, but really, in my many years running this bookshop, I've learnt that there is no rhyme or reason to it.'

'But surely there are trends,' said Jemma. 'Lots of new books are released in September, and then there's the run-up to Christmas—'

'Not in this bookshop,' said Raphael. 'I think it's time for elevenses. Would you mind doing the honours?'

Jemma went through to the back room, switched on the kettle, and found that they were out of Raphael's favourite Earl Grey teabags. 'I don't believe it,' she muttered. 'I swear the shop is out to get me.' She remembered the article that Em had sent her, and shivered. 'He'll have to make do with ordinary,' she told herself, dropping three teabags into the pot. She felt somewhat less sanguine when she saw Raphael's face as he took the first sip of his tea.

She could bear it no longer. 'About the trial period—'

'Oh yes,' said Raphael, putting his cup down precisely in the saucer. 'It's been very nice having you here.' Then he returned to his newspaper.

Oh, thought Jemma. *I guess that's it then*. She felt as if she had had a rug pulled from under her but nothing else had changed. 'I suppose you want your cookbook back, then.'

'Only when you've finished with it,' said Raphael, filling in a clue on the crossword.

'I don't have it with me today,' said Jemma. 'I'll – I'll bring it in next week.'

'Oh yes, you do that,' said Raphael, not looking up.

'I'm just going into the stockroom,' said Jemma. Receiving no response, she bolted, and presently found herself staring at the aisles of boxes. *What do I do now?*

The blank boxes stared back at her.

Jemma searched through her memories of all the courses she had attended and all the blog posts she had read for some nuggets of wisdom. 'What can I learn from this experience?' she whispered.

'You could ask for feedback,' said a helpful little voice which sounded rather like Em's.

Oh God, I'll have to tell Em that I only lasted a week. I'll ask for feedback on what I did wrong, and promise to do better, and ask for another week's trial. Jemma took several deep breaths, then went back into the main shop. 'Could I ask for your feedback, please?'

She spoke louder than she had intended, and Raphael almost jumped out of the armchair. Folio, who was sitting on his lap, rearranged himself with a baleful glare at Jemma. She was getting used to Folio's baleful glare, though, so that didn't worry her too much.

'Feedback?' said Raphael. 'About what?'

'About my performance this week,' said Jemma. 'Because if there are things I've done that you weren't happy with, or that I could have done better, I'd welcome the opportunity to learn from you, and perhaps we could do another week's trial?' She gave him her best enthusiastic smile.

Raphael stared at her in disbelief, then started laughing. 'You haven't done anything wrong,' he choked out eventually. 'The shop hasn't burnt down, and we still have all the books, and there haven't been any riots so far this week.'

'That's a fairly low bar,' said Jemma.

'You haven't met some of my assistants,' said Raphael darkly. 'There was one time when I had to escape in a kayak. And no, I don't want to talk about it.'

'So . . . does that mean I can stay?' said Jemma.

'I don't see why not,' said Raphael. 'Folio seems to like you.'

Jemma looked at Folio, whose glare had softened to topaz inscrutability.

'Do you still have all your fingers?' Jemma held them up. 'Exactly,' said Raphael. 'And the shop seems to like you. Most of the time.'

It was on the tip of Jemma's tongue to ask how a shop could possibly have feelings; but she sensed that now was not the right time to voice such a thought. 'That's good, then,' she said, rather weakly. 'If you like, I could show you some projections I've put together, based on the recommendations in the action plan I drew up—'

'That won't be necessary,' said Raphael. 'Just keep doing what you're doing. And perhaps not too much of that.'

'Too much of what?' asked Jemma.

'You know,' said Raphael. He waved a hand. 'The spreadsheety, projectiony, computery thing.'

'The computery thing,' said Jemma. 'All right, I'll do less of the computery thing.' She resolved to do computery things when he wasn't watching, as they seemed to be working. 'But I can stay?'

'Of course you may stay,' said Raphael, sounding surprised. 'You're the first assistant I've had since – well, I can't remember – who has lasted till Friday.'

Jemma felt a slight prickle of unease. 'Why is that, do you think?'

Raphael considered, gazing into the middle distance, or possibly at the Self Help section. 'Oh, there are many reasons which I won't bother you with just yet. I really don't think it will be relevant. Now, would you like to ask me again if you can stay, or may I get on with my crossword?'

Jemma opened and closed her mouth like a fish out of water.

'We can sign something, if it would make you feel better,' said Raphael. He got up, went to the counter, and pulled a brown-paper bag off the string. Then he took a fountain pen out of his jacket pocket and wrote rapidly on the paper. 'Here.' He held it out to Jemma.

Jemma read what he had written in his beautiful copperplate.

I, Raphael Burns, promise to employ Jemma James at Burns Books for as long as it is mutually convenient to us both.

I, Jemma James, agree to work in said bookshop until I am bored or for other reasons.

Raphael had already signed it. 'Will that do?' he said.

Jemma thought of early mornings clutching a cup of grainy coffee from the kiosk by the tube, hurrying home in the evening via Kris's Takeaway, and waking up in the middle of the night convinced she had left something vital out of her latest report.

'It'll do,' she said. Raphael passed her his fountain pen, she signed with her little flourish, and the deed was done.

Jemma's clock radio woke her with 'Fame' on Monday morning, which she took as an exceptionally good omen. Not that she wanted to be famous – good heavens, no – except perhaps as some sort of shop turnaround-er, like Mary Portas. Yes, that would be good. Maybe she could have her own series, going into unprofitable businesses and, with a wave of her magic wand, transforming them into happy places where the money poured in. She decided to have wholemeal toast with organic strawberry jam for breakfast. After all, it was an important day.

Today the tube didn't misbehave, and Jemma arrived at Burns Books at a quarter past eight. It was a lovely bright spring day, but with a fresh breeze and a slight chill in the air which she hoped would induce chilly tourists to pop in for a browse. *A day to blow the cobwebs away*, she thought. *Oh, what a good idea*. She delved into her bag and brought out her new prized possession: the keys to the shop.

Raphael had given them to her after closing on Friday. 'Would you mind opening up on Monday?' he asked. 'I always find Mondays rather difficult.'

'Yes, of course,' Jemma said, watching the keys as they swung gently back and forth on Raphael's finger.

'Now, the big iron key is for the lock which is under the handle,' said Raphael. 'It's a bit stiff. And the other lock is at eye level.' He studied Jemma. 'Actually, you might need to look up.'

'I'm sure I can manage,' said Jemma, taking the keys off his finger. *I'll get a keyring for them*, she thought. *Something bookish. I wonder if we could sell keyrings in the shop?* She resolved to follow that up at the weekend.

And she had, as well as planning the bookshop's social media content for the next three months, and producing a set of graphs showing which genres had sold best over the previous week. She had also bought herself another pair of baseball boots, an extra pair of smartish trousers, this time in navy, and, on impulse, a T-shirt which said *Bookworm And Proud* in curved rainbow lettering. It was a bit children's TV presenter, but she figured that sending a clear message was part of her communication strategy.

She had also found time to send a quick text to Em. *Had my review yesterday and I'm permanent in the shop. Can't wait to get properly started.*

And she couldn't. Not even when Em replied: *Are you sure you're doing the right thing? I just don't see how this can be a career X.*

I can, and that's what matters. And with that Jemma put her phone out of reach, and carried on with her trend analysis.

But I have to get back to basics first, she thought, as she jiggled the huge iron key in the lock. *I have to get into the shop, and open it up.*

The lock finally gave in, and admitted her. The Yale lock, by comparison, was a doddle, though she did have to stand on tiptoe to get a good view of it. The door swung open, and the bright, merciless light revealed the state of the shop.

'I'm here!' she called, but there was no response. Not even a meow.

Oh my, she thought, as cobwebs wafted gently in the breeze. *The shop looks as if it's been asleep for a thousand years. And it's only been a weekend.* She heaved a sigh, then winced as a cobweb settled on her face. She batted it away, then frowned. *If there are this many cobwebs, then how many spiders must there be? And how many flies?* She shuddered, and pulled up the blind to reveal a decidedly grimy shop window.

'You need cleaning, and no mistake,' she said, nodding at it. 'I'll open up, and then I shall deal with you.' She ran a fingertip over the window, and grimaced at the result.

There was plenty of change in the till, even though Jemma had made Raphael go to the bank with a large bundle of cash on Friday afternoon, and she switched the lights on without any untoward incidents. *In some ways*, she thought, surveying the premises, *it might be better to leave them switched off.* The additional light emphasised the dust which rose every time Jemma moved around, and gave the cobwebs shadows which made them seem twice as thick. *Right,* she thought, *I'd better get to it. I've got about half an hour before the shop is supposed to be ready for customers.*

Jemma looked for a bucket, but drew a blank. *How does he clean this place?* Then she tried the cupboard under the sink in the back room for cleaning materials, but found nothing. She decided to assume that Raphael kept such things in his own flat above the shop. The alternative was too depressing to imagine. In the end she commandeered the washing-up bowl, which she filled with hot water and a squirt of washing-up liquid in the absence of anything better, and grabbed a J-cloth from the side of the sink. She made a mental note to research natural cleaning products, and carried the bowl through to the front of the shop.

I'd better start at the top, she thought, and fetched the small step which she used for restocking the middle shelves. Then she cleared out the window display, which needed redoing anyway, and set to work.

She was stretching into the top right-hand corner of the window when a cough nearly sent her into space. 'What are you doing?' enquired Raphael.

'What do you think I'm doing?' Jemma replied.

Raphael said nothing for a moment, but gazed at the window. 'I heard squeaking,' he said.

'That,' said Jemma, wringing her cloth out, 'is the sound of clean.' She gestured at the bowl. 'Look at the state of that water.'

Raphael frowned. 'Why are you using dirty water to

wash the window?'

'It wasn't dirty when I started,' said Jemma, between gritted teeth. 'Where do you keep your cleaning stuff?'

'I need a coffee,' said Raphael. 'And it needs to be an espresso.'

'Not like that, I hope,' said Jemma, eyeing his dressing gown.

Raphael looked down at himself, and seemed surprised. 'Good point,' he said, and disappeared, returning a very short time later in a surprisingly normal combination of cream linen trousers and a white shirt. 'Back soon,' he said, and loped off. As he opened the door the bell rang, and a fine mist of dust floated down.

'I give up,' said Jemma. 'No, I don't. I am going to get this filthy shop clean if it kills me.'

Outside, the sun went behind a cloud.

'That's actually an improvement,' said Jemma, and faced the window again.

A few minutes later the window was, if not sparkling, not noticeably dirty. On the inside, at least. Jemma looked at her watch. Fifteen minutes until opening time. *I can nip out and do the outside as well*, she thought. *With fresh water*. Whistling, she went to refill her bowl, and found that, without knowing it, she had managed to use all the washing-up liquid. *Well, hot water is better than nothing.*

Ten minutes later Jemma re-entered the shop, reasonably pleased with the state of the window, and found Folio chewing the broom which had been part of her Harry Potter window display.

'That's a good idea, Folio,' she said. 'If I can't wash the

floor, at least I can sweep it.' She knelt and attempted to take the broom from Folio, but he responded by leaping on top of the bristles and digging his claws into the wooden handle.

'If you won't let go,' said Jemma, 'then I'll have to sweep the floor with you as well.' She picked up the broom by the end of the handle, since she didn't like the look of Folio's claws, and took it to the back of the shop.

'I think Raphael is overfeeding you,' she said to Folio as she wielded the broom. 'You really are a bit heavy for a cat.'

Folio hissed, and attempted to swipe at her.

She had swept most of the dust to the front of the shop when Raphael returned. 'If you hold the door for me,' said Jemma, breathlessly, 'I'll just sweep all this outside, and then we can open.'

Raphael raised his eyebrows. 'Aren't you going to clean the window first?'

Jemma followed his pointing finger and saw that within the last few minutes, the entire local bird population had used the shop window for target practice. Her jaw dropped, and the breeze from the open shop door blew a long thread of cobweb into her mouth. 'Ugh!' she exclaimed, trying to spit it out.

'I'll deal with the window,' said Raphael soothingly. 'You go and get a drink of water.'

'I need something stronger than water,' muttered Jemma.

When she returned from the back room, having taken several deep breaths to calm herself, the window was clean again, and somehow the shop seemed considerably less dirty. Raphael had procured a feather duster from somewhere, and was winding cobwebs around it like candy floss. Folio had abandoned the broom, and was sitting in the shop window between copies of *Catwatching* and *The Unadulterated Cat*. A couple stopped, pointed at Folio, then entered the shop.

Jemma's fists clenched automatically, and she uncurled them with an effort. 'Good morning, how can I help you?' she said, stepping forward. *Don't think you've won,* she told the shop, in her head. *I'm not going to be beaten by a shop with a mind of its own. And if you think this is over, you are so wrong.*

She felt something drop on the back of her neck and scuttle under her top, but her smile, now rather forced, never left her face.

The rest of the morning passed without incident, possibly because Jemma confined herself to normal duties such as restocking the bookshelves and serving the customers. *Perhaps I tried to do too much*, she thought. *It was a bit ambitious for a Monday morning.* The sun came back out, and Folio spent his morning reclining in the shop window, shifting himself along every so often to stay in the sunshine. Jemma found a box of books on pet care in the stockroom, put them in the window, and sold half the box within an hour.

'Have you trained him to do that?' asked a woman in cycling gear, nodding at Folio.

'Do what?' said Jemma.

'Stay in the window like that.'

Raphael came to join them. 'Folio is very much his own cat,' he said. 'He does as he pleases.'

Folio opened a lazy yellow eye, regarded them all, and closed it again with a contented whiffle.

It was a pleasant morning, but truth be told, Jemma found it dull. *What about my action plan? How will I implement it if the shop is determined to thwart me at every turn?* Then she laughed. *Listen to yourself, Jemma James. This is a shop. An inanimate object. It's all just – coincidence.* She went to get more books from the stockroom, tripped over the broom which definitely hadn't been there before, and almost went flying.

'Steady now,' said Raphael, grabbing her arm. 'I don't want to have to use the first-aid kit.'

'I'm glad to hear you've got one,' Jemma said grumpily, as she had stubbed her toe.

'I think we have,' said Raphael. 'It sounds like the sort of thing a shop ought to have.'

'Yes, it does,' said Jemma, hoping that her stern expression would prompt Raphael to go and look for said kit and thereby prove that it existed. Given that morning's experience in the shop, she had a feeling that a well-stocked first-aid kit was an essential item.

Raphael opened the cupboard under the sink and pulled out a square green box with a white cross on the lid. 'Here we are,' he said. 'I knew we had one somewhere.'

'But that wasn't—' Jemma stopped. Certainly she hadn't noticed a first-aid kit when she had searched for cleaning materials that morning, but that didn't mean it hadn't been there. It was just that she hadn't been looking for it. Of course, that was it. There was no other explanation. None at all.

Raphael gave the lid of the box a pat and put it back into the cupboard. 'Good to know it's there,' he said. 'One never knows, does one.' He gave Jemma a stern look of his own. 'But it still pays to be careful. Health and safety, you know.'

'That's a point,' said Jemma. 'Is there a course I should go on?'

Raphael shivered, though the temperature in the shop must have been at least twenty degrees. 'I hardly think that's necessary,' he said. 'Really, it's a matter of common sense, isn't it. Staying out of trouble. Avoiding temptation. Not – not overdoing things.' From his serious expression, Jemma gathered that she was supposed to be deriving wisdom from these vague comments.

'That is true,' she said. 'But nothing ventured, nothing gained.' She went into the stockroom, and closed the door behind her.

I can't believe he's lecturing me, she thought. *Raphael, who barely knows one end of the till from the other! The shop's profits have gone up by . . . a lot since I started working here.* She pulled out the first box she saw, reopened the door with difficulty, and carried it through to the counter. When she opened the box, the book on top was *Accidents at Work: A survey of the most common workplace injuries, with notes on how to avoid them.*

Jemma dropped it on the counter. 'Very funny,' she muttered. Beneath it was a copy of *Howards End*. Jemma reached into the box, lifted out a stack of books, and moved around the shop shelving them.

As she slid the last book into the Biography section,

Raphael wandered through. 'I might go for lunch,' he said vaguely. 'Would you mind if I left you alone in the shop for an hour or so?'

Jemma folded her arms, mainly to stop herself rubbing her hands with glee. Until now, Raphael had never left her alone in the shop for more than twenty minutes or so. 'Oh, sure,' she said casually. 'That'll be fine. I'll pick something up when you get back.'

'Excellent,' said Raphael. 'I'll be in Rolando's if you need me. You know, the deli?'

Jemma knew. After all, she passed it every day when she came to work, and again when she left. It was always busy, and a delicious aroma of coffee and baking seeped out every time the door opened. As yet she hadn't ventured in, suspecting that acquiring a deli habit would eat into her slim salary and expand her waistline. She could get an egg mayonnaise sandwich from the mini-market for a pound, anyway.

'Jemma…'

She came to and saw Raphael looking at her curiously. 'Yes, what is it?' she asked, cross at being caught daydreaming.

'You aren't planning to do anything while I'm out, are you?'

'Who, me?' Jemma laughed. 'The thought hadn't even entered my head.'

'Good,' said Raphael. He smiled. 'I find, with the shop, that it's best to introduce things gradually. Nothing too . . . surprising.'

'Oh yes,' said Jemma. 'Incremental steps. Continuous

improvement. Kaizen.'

'Bless you,' said Raphael, and left.

Once the shop door had closed behind him Jemma went into the back room, stretched out her arms, and spun around. She wasn't sure why being alone in the shop gave her such joy, especially after this morning's shenanigans, but it did. *Perhaps one day I shall have a shop of my own*, she thought, *and I'll arrange it just as I like*. Then the shop bell rang, and she hurried into the shop to assist the next customer.

A stream of customers came into the shop over the next hour. Some wanted travel guides to plan for their holidays. Some were thinking of getting a kitten or a puppy, and were researching different breeds. One even asked whether marmalade cats like Folio were easy to live with. Jemma, now in an excellent mood, replied, 'We get along fine. But he isn't my cat, he's the bookshop cat.'

Folio leapt onto the counter and sat with his paws together, looking extremely pleased with himself. The customer asked if she could take his picture.

At one point there was even a queue. *Imagine that*, thought Jemma. She wondered if it would be rude to ask whether she could take a picture of the line, to show Raphael, and decided regretfully that it would. *He'll be stunned when I tell him*, she thought, putting two twenty-pound notes into the right compartment in the till, and getting change. *Maybe we can set a new record for takings today. That would be something.* She saw herself putting today's number into her spreadsheet, and watching the trend line adjust itself upwards.

Eventually the rush died down, and the shop bell was quiet. Jemma checked her watch. It was a quarter to two. *Raphael's having a long lunch*, she thought, and tried not to feel resentful. Her stomach growled in agreement, and she patted it. 'Don't worry, you'll be fed,' she said. 'Given what a profitable morning it's been, I might treat you to lunch from the deli today. I think it's time for a change from egg mayo.'

She surveyed the shop from her vantage point behind the counter. Despite all the customers, everything was spick and span. She needed to get more stock out, of course, but—

Her eye fell on an envelope which was sitting on the doormat.

Funny time for the post, thought Jemma. Then again, she hadn't taken notice of what time it usually came. She went over and picked the envelope up.

It was a long white envelope, unstamped, with *BURNS BOOKS* written on it in block capitals.

How odd, thought Jemma. She slid her thumb under the flap, then stopped. *Should I open it?* But why not? It wasn't addressed specifically to Raphael, but to the bookshop. It didn't say *Private*, and it didn't look official.

Maybe it's a fan letter, she thought, letting her imagination run wild. *Maybe it's a thank-you letter from one of our customers. Or it could be someone searching for a special book, like Helene Hanff.* She imagined a handsome stranger writing from somewhere she'd like to visit; Barcelona, or Lisbon, or Paris. He would be seeking a specific edition of… She looked at the shelves for inspiration. *Great Expectations*. And she would reply, enclosing the book, and they would court each other by letter—

Folio yowled, and Jemma jumped. She ripped open the envelope, displeased to be brought back to stone-cold reality.

Inside was a sheet of A4 paper, folded in three. Jemma opened it out, and stared.

It wasn't a fan letter.

It wasn't a thank-you letter.

And it wasn't a request for a specific edition of *Great Expectations*, or any other of Dickens's works.

The text had been cut from newspapers and magazines.

I kNOw WhAt yOu'Re uP To, AND i'M gOiNg tO StOP yOu. fOr GooD.

Jemma blinked, then read the letter again. If anything, it made even less sense the second time. *What the—*

She let the letter fall on the counter, and shivered. Suddenly the shop seemed cold, and there was a strange, musty, heavy smell in the air.

The bell jangled. Jemma snatched up the note and put it behind her back before realising that it was Raphael. He looked concerned. 'Is everything all right?' he asked. 'I – I felt I should pop in and check.'

Jemma replaced the letter on the counter and shook her head. 'No,' she said. 'The shop has had a letter. We've had a letter. An anonymous letter.'

Raphael dived for the letter, scanned it, then screwed it up in a ball and put it in his pocket. 'Just someone being silly,' he said. 'Don't worry about it.'

Jemma frowned. *When have I seen him do that before?*

Then she remembered him sifting through the post on her first day in the shop. 'This isn't the first, is it?'

Raphael said nothing, but jammed his hands into his pockets and shifted from foot to foot.

'So it isn't,' said Jemma, folding her arms.

'No, it isn't,' said Raphael. 'But it really isn't anything to worry about.'

'Have you phoned the police?' asked Jemma. 'What did the first note say?'

'No, I haven't phoned the police,' said Raphael. 'I don't think it would do any good to have the police round here asking questions. And I can't remember what the first note even said. I threw it in the bin.' His brow furrowed. 'To my recollection, it was pretty much like this one.'

'But someone's threatening you!' cried Jemma. 'That's serious.'

'People can threaten all they like,' said Raphael. 'They can't do anything. What could they do?'

Jemma shrugged. 'I don't know,' she said.

'Exactly,' said Raphael, and the atmosphere in the shop lightened a bit. 'Just empty threats.' He reached into his coat pocket and held out a paper bag. 'I brought you a panini. Cheese and ham.'

'Oh. Thank you,' said Jemma as she took it. She managed a wavering smile. 'Who do you think sent the letter?'

'Not a clue,' said Raphael. 'And what's more, I don't care. Now, why don't you make a nice cup of tea to go with that panini.'

Jemma went through to the back room and put the

kettle on. She tried to think of nice things like serving customers and putting money into the till, but the note, with its cut-out lettering and its vague threat, kept getting in the way. *He clearly doesn't want to talk about it*, she thought, putting teabags into the pot. *And he won't call the police.* She sighed. *So there's nothing I can do.*

She felt pressure against her legs, and looked down to find Folio rubbing his head on her ankle. 'Good cat,' she said absentmindedly, and reached down to stroke him. When her hand was within clawing range she wondered if that was a good idea, but Folio accepted the fuss readily enough, and even managed a throaty purr.

'Gooooood cat,' Jemma purred back, feeling much less troubled. Raphael was right. It was an empty threat. She could barely remember what the letter had said.

She made the tea, took it through, and enjoyed the luxury of eating her panini in the armchair while Raphael counted the morning's takings. 'Excellent,' he said. 'The shop *is* doing well,' and Jemma felt a little ember of pride warm her through. The sun had come back, lending a pleasing glow to the mahogany counter and the parquet floor, and the shop did look very nice indeed.

Everything went swimmingly, in fact, until Raphael let out a groan. Then he jumped up and strode into the back room, calling over his shoulder, 'If he asks to see me, tell him I'm dead. Or travelling the world. Or otherwise engaged.'

'If who asks to see you?' said Jemma.

'I don't know who you're talking to,' Raphael shouted. 'I'm not here.'

The door opened, and a smiley man in a short-sleeved shirt, beige chinos and a tie came in. He was holding a clipboard. 'Could you spare me a moment?' he asked.

'Um, probably,' said Jemma. He seemed harmless enough.

'First of all, I don't suppose your boss happens to be about, does he?' He consulted his clipboard. 'Mr, ah, Burns.'

'I'm afraid he's busy in the stockroom,' said Jemma, crossing her fingers under the counter. Raphael might well be in the stockroom, and possibly busy.

'Oh, I see.' The smile became even more open and friendly. 'Could you pop through and ask if he's got time for a word?'

Jemma shook her head. 'I can't leave the shop unattended.'

The man nodded. 'Quite right too. In that case, I'll introduce myself. My name is Richard Tennant, and I'm from the Westminster Retailers' Association, Charing Cross Branch.' He extended a large hand.

Before Jemma could shake it, Raphael erupted from the back room. 'Don't waste your breath, Tennant,' he said, taking up position behind the counter next to Jemma. 'I'm not joining your stupid association. Not now, not ever.'

Mr Tennant looked rather hurt. 'That's a real shame, Mr Burns. Our membership on Charing Cross Road is higher than ever, and we're getting to the point where the association has a real voice. Strength in numbers, and all that.'

Raphael looked down his long nose at him. 'To

61

paraphrase Groucho Marx,' he said, 'I wouldn't join any association that wanted me for a member.'

Mr Tennant chuckled. 'Very droll, Mr Burns, very droll. Well, I see I won't be able to convince you today, so I'll leave you our latest newsletter and be on my way.' He unclipped a colourful pamphlet from his board and laid it on the counter. 'Perhaps I should add that many of the bookshops in this area are finding it beneficial. Anyway, if you do change your mind, you know where to find me.'

'Thank you so much,' said Raphael coldly. And as Mr Tennant turned to go, Raphael picked up the newsletter and, very deliberately, tore it in half. Mr Tennant's shoulders stiffened slightly, but he kept walking, and left without another word.

'What was all that about?' asked Jemma, once the door had closed behind him. 'Why don't you like him? And why wouldn't we want to join a retail association? Surely that would be good for us.'

'Not if they start telling me what to do,' muttered Raphael, tearing the newsletter into long strips. 'Not if they start saying the shop has to conform to this or that regulation. I'll – I'll sell the shop before I let some chirpy chap with a clipboard tell me what's what.' He picked up the wastepaper basket and swept the strips of paper into it, scowling. 'I need pastry,' he said, and stalked out.

Back to Rolando's, I presume, thought Jemma, with a sigh. She eyed the shelves, which looked distinctly gappy, and hurried to the stockroom for more books. When she opened the boxes, she found an assortment of novels by Len Deighton and Robert Ludlum. Yet they hadn't sold any spy thrillers that morning, as far as she remembered.

I wonder why he is so against the retail association, she thought, as she began to shelve the books. *I mean, I can see it would be a good thing. He could learn from the other booksellers. And I doubt they would tell him what to do.*

Then a sneaky little thought almost made her drop *The Bourne Identity. Maybe Raphael doesn't want to join because he doesn't want anyone to know what he's doing. And that note said he was up to something.*

She slid the book into place, and reached for another. *But what, exactly, is he up to?*

Chapter 9

Jemma mused as she shelved books. What could Raphael be up to? She was half tempted to nip to Rolando's and peek in at the window to see if he really was there.

But he was there earlier, her rational brain said. *He brought you a panini, remember?*

It takes, what, three minutes to buy a panini? He could have popped in after he'd been doing – whatever he had been doing.

It could be something perfectly innocent, she told herself. *Raphael might have some sort of side hustle.*

Or he could be – I don't know – smuggling, or money-laundering? On impulse, Jemma opened the till and looked inside. While the shop's takings were definitely up from the heady heights of the fifty pounds that Raphael had mentioned, there definitely wasn't enough cash in there to fuel anyone's suspicions of money laundering. Jemma closed the till drawer, which snapped shut with its usual satisfying chime. Yet she remained unsatisfied.

'The stockroom,' she muttered. 'All those unlabelled boxes. Anything could be in them.' On impulse she went into the stockroom and picked up a few boxes to test their weight. To be perfectly honest, they all felt about the right weight to be boxes of books, and with some gentle shaking, they sounded like books, too.

Whatever he's doing, thought Jemma as she closed the stockroom door, *I don't think it relates to the shop.* Then she remembered how the shop had chilled when she read the anonymous letter. She tried to dismiss it as a coincidence. But frankly, there had been a lot of similar coincidences. Including the way that the air had thinned and the musty smell had vanished when Raphael dismissed the letter as nonsense.

'You'll start reading your horoscope next,' she said aloud, and snorted. Actually… The newspaper was folded on the counter where Raphael had left it. Jemma opened it and found the horoscope section.

TAURUS: Today will be a day of ups and downs, but beware of jumping to conclusions. A mysterious stranger will bring you something of value.

Jemma harrumphed, refolded the paper, and put it back. *That was probably Raphael bringing me a panini. I bet they're expensive.* Or could it mean Mr Tennant from the Charing Cross Retail Association, who had brought that newsletter? She rummaged in the bin, and began to piece it together.

She was reading the newsletter when Raphael returned, looking much happier. 'Any customers?' he enquired.

'None, actually,' said Jemma. 'I'm just reading that newsletter you ripped up.'

A pained expression passed over Raphael's face. 'What rare gems have you discovered?' he asked.

'They're talking to landlords about lowering shop rents,' said Jemma. 'That's good, isn't it?'

'It would be,' said Raphael. 'But I happen to own the shop, so that doesn't apply to me.'

'Oh yes,' said Jemma. 'I forgot.' She eyed Raphael. 'So, how long have you been in charge of the shop?'

'Oh, years,' said Raphael. 'Ages.'

'Like, in the last century?' asked Jemma. She studied him. There wasn't any grey in his sandy hair, but he didn't seem young. And she couldn't get any clues from the way he dressed. She suspected Raphael was one of those people who had always looked middle-aged, and always would.

Raphael laughed. 'Are you trying to work out how old I am?'

'No,' said Jemma. 'OK, maybe.'

'That's a bit cheeky,' said Raphael, but he didn't seem annoyed.

'Sorry,' said Jemma. 'I suppose I'm curious because I don't know anything about you.'

Raphael raised his eyebrows. 'I've told you my name, and you know that this is my shop, and I live above it. What else is there?'

'All sorts of things,' said Jemma. 'What music you

listen to, what you like to do in your spare time. What you did before you inherited the shop.'

'Oh, I see,' said Raphael. 'What do you like to do in your spare time?'

'Oh, well…' Jemma thought for a while. 'I suppose I don't really have any.'

'How come?' Jemma wondered briefly if Raphael was attempting to distract her, but he appeared genuinely interested.

'Well, in my last job I got into the habit of working long hours, and…' She tried to think of a way to put a positive spin on her lack of a private life. 'I'm very driven, you see,' she said. 'Even when I'm not in the shop, I'm thinking of ways to improve the shop. New initiatives, exciting window displays. That sort of thing.'

The pained expression returned. 'You don't have to try so hard, Jemma,' Raphael said gently.

'But what's the point of having a shop if it isn't successful?' Jemma asked. 'I mean, look how your sales have increased! Look how much money there is in the till! When I first came, you weren't even making fifty pounds a day.' She opened the till, took out a wad of notes, and shook them at him.

Raphael didn't quite recoil from the money, but he regarded it with a troubled air. 'How much have you got there, do you think?'

Jemma began counting the notes. When she got to four hundred Raphael said quietly, 'That will do.'

'See?' said Jemma, putting the money into the till. 'You won't even let me implement my plan fully, but it's

67

working. The shop is doing better than – probably than it ever has. But I feel that I have to make the effort, because *you* won't.' *There*, she thought triumphantly. *I've said it. If that doesn't get him on board, I don't know what will.*

'But before you came, the shop had been here for generations,' said Raphael. 'The shop existed before Charing Cross Road was built. That's how old it is. In living memory, there has always been a Burns Books. So we must have been doing something right.'

'Oh, I didn't mean you've been doing things wrong,' Jemma said kindly. 'I didn't mean that at all. But—'

'The shop has been here so long,' said Raphael, 'because it knows its place. Among the other shops, and particularly the bookshops. Every shop has its own character, its own specialism, and its own particular set of customers. It's a delicate balance, and upsetting it might have consequences.'

'Like a sort of business ecosystem, you mean?' said Jemma. 'I read a blog about that last year.' She frowned. 'So what is our specialism? I thought we sold all types of books.'

'Oh, we do,' said Raphael. 'The distinction is subtler than that. When you've worked here a bit longer, you'll be able to identify it for yourself.' He smiled. 'Tea?' And without waiting for an answer, he went through to the back room.

Jemma gathered up the torn strips of newsletter and dropped them into the bin. It seemed pretty clear that, whatever the benefits, Raphael wasn't ever going to join the Charing Cross Retail Association. She remembered his plea to her not to do the spreadsheety computery things. Her brow furrowed. 'But if I don't do those,' she murmured, 'then why am I here? Anyone could put books on the shelves, then put them into bags for the customers and take the money. If I can't bring my own particular skill set to the job, then what's the point?'

Folio leapt onto the counter and nuzzled into her elbow.

'That's very kind,' said Jemma, stroking his head. 'I appreciate it.' She let out a heavy sigh. 'Perhaps I should take up a hobby. Civil War battle re-enactments, or crochet, or something.' She considered checking the Hobbies section, but Folio flopped down and lifted his chin for a tickle, and it would have been rude to ignore him.

'Here we are,' said Raphael, coming through with a tray. 'The cup that cheers but not inebriates.' He looked at Folio, who looked back at him upside down. 'Good heavens.'

'Maybe he does like me,' said Jemma, and felt a little bit better. But as Raphael busied himself pouring out, two quite different thoughts popped into her head.

The first thought was that he hadn't answered any of her questions. Not with anything you could call detail, or specifics.

And the second thought was that, even though she wasn't happy with the idea of just being a normal shop assistant, and of course she *could* walk out and get a role more suitable to her talents whenever she liked, the thought of looking for another job hadn't crossed her mind. Not once.

Chapter 10

Jemma was quiet for the rest of the day; so much so that Raphael asked if she was feeling all right.

'What?' she said. 'Oh yes, just thinking.'

And Jemma was thinking. She thought as she walked down Charing Cross Road at five minutes past five, as she touched in at Embankment tube station, as she swayed from a strap in the train, and as she let herself into her flat.

Nebulous thoughts swirled around her brain.

What do I do if I can't improve the shop?

What do I do if I don't want a different job?

What can I do?

She had no answers to the questions yet. They just continued to echo in her head in a disquieting manner. And that was the main problem. She had absolutely no idea what to do.

I don't understand, she thought. *I always know what to*

do. I apply the lessons I've learned through training, or I do research, or I work harder. But I've tried that with Raphael. I've tried every trick in the book, and none of them seem to work.

She thought of Phoebe, her former boss, with affection. Even when things hadn't gone to plan Phoebe always had a suggestion, or would agree with what Jemma proposed. The second was what she generally did, and Jemma appreciated it. It showed that Phoebe valued her opinion.

But Phoebe had let her go. She had said it was a business decision and not a personal one; but she had still let her go.

Jemma sighed, went through to the kitchen, and looked through the *Easy Suppers* cookbook for something which would challenge her. If she couldn't achieve her potential in the workplace, she'd darn well hone her skills somewhere else.

An hour and a half later Jemma sat down to four ramekins, each containing a cheese soufflé at a different stage of deflation. If anything, she felt slightly more frustrated than she had when she started cooking.

'But what do I do?' she said, through a mouthful of soggy soufflé.

Two soufflés in, Jemma decided her need for clarity was stronger than her need for further cheese-based sustenance. In a fit of desperation she fetched the tote bag she had brought home from her previous job, hung up on the back of the door, and forgotten about. She couldn't even remember what was in there, but perhaps there was something that could help. She rummaged within, and found a pen and two packs of company-branded Post-it notes. 'Why on earth did I put those in?' she said, staring at them. Never mind; they would do.

Jemma sat down at the little drop-leaf table she used for eating and working, clicked her pen, and began to write.

Problem: Raphael won't let me do things. After some thought, she added: *Why?*

'Of course! The Five Whys technique!' she cried. 'Why didn't I think of that before?' She almost started writing that before she realised it wasn't a relevant Why. She pulled off the first Post-it note and stuck it on the table.

He doesn't want to upset the balance of the business ecosystem, she wrote on the next note. She stuck it on the table and regarded it for some time. 'Do you really believe that?' she asked herself.

On the next note she wrote: *Maybe he doesn't trust me. Why?*

The next notes were much easier.

Maybe because I'm new.

Maybe because he's worried I'll mess up.

Maybe because he's worried I'll take over the shop. She considered that final point; she had to admit that it was an attractive prospect. 'OK, fair enough,' she said. 'You've got me on that one, Raphael.'

On the next note, she wrote simply: *What can I do?* She stretched and stuck that on the far side of the table. Underneath it she placed the following:

Continue to implement small-scale quick wins to build R's trust in me.

Wait until I've been there longer before suggesting

more improvements.

Focus on something else to lull his suspicions.

Jemma sat back, folded her arms, and regarded the last note. It didn't convey the message that she wanted, which was one of mild diversion rather than all-out subterfuge, but she had a feeling that it might work.

'I'll persuade him,' she said slowly, 'that finding out who's behind the anonymous letters is a good idea. That will help me to learn more about the shop, more about the people who come in, and possibly more about Raphael.' *And what he's up to*, she thought to herself.

Pleased with her proposed course of action, Jemma wrote another note, *Find the anonymous letter-writer*, and stuck it at the head of the table, then rearranged the other Post-it notes into a hierarchy. She considered starting a spreadsheet, then thought that might be overkill, seeing as she needed to win Raphael over first.

She sighed with satisfaction and dug her spoon into the last cheese soufflé, which was now cold and tasted like a cheese puff that had been dropped into a bucket of water. *Rome wasn't built in a day*, she thought.

***

The next day, Jemma dressed in what she thought of as her least professional and most unthreatening outfit: a pair of faded jeans, her baseball boots, and a plain pale-blue T-shirt. 'The psychology of dress is very important,' she said, nodding to her reflection in the mirror and slouching a little.

She didn't get her usual tube train, setting off twenty minutes later than she normally would, and arriving at the shop at an unprecedented five minutes past nine. 'Sorry I'm late,' she said cheerily. 'Rush-hour. You know.'

'I'm not sure I do,' said Raphael, but he appeared rather relieved. 'If you get the kettle on, I'll open up.'

'Righto,' said Jemma, and made sure that she brewed Raphael's Earl Grey to the required strength.

They had a couple of customers first thing; two smartly dressed women in late middle age who weren't together, but were both looking for Golden Age crime. Jemma packed up a selection of Agatha Christie, Ngaio Marsh, and Gladys Mitchell for them, and wrote the shop's phone number on their bags. The two customers also swapped their phone numbers and left together, chatting.

'That was nice,' said Raphael. 'I like to think that we're bringing readers together.'

It was on the tip of Jemma's tongue to suggest that they start genre-specific book clubs, and perhaps a customer network, but she bit it back. Instead she took in the atmosphere of the shop. It was pleasantly warm and bright today, and the sometimes harsh spring sunshine had mellowed to a comforting glow.

'If you don't mind,' she said, 'I might polish the counter.'

Raphael stared at her. 'I suppose you could,' he said doubtfully. 'You'll find polish and a duster under the sink.'

Jemma smiled to herself as she went into the back room. The polish and duster were right at the front of the cupboard. She went through, sprayed polish on the counter and rubbed it in, working with light, smooth strokes, and following the grain of the wood.

Folio, who was sitting on the chair arm, rolled onto his back, presenting Raphael with his tummy.

'I was wondering,' said Jemma, continuing to rub. 'You know the letter that came?'

Raphael looked across at her, one hand poised above Folio's belly. 'Yes?'

'Would you mind,' said Jemma, 'if I made some discreet enquiries?'

Raphael said nothing. Folio was motionless. The shop seemed to be waiting.

'You see,' said Jemma, 'I think stuff like that brings bad vibes to the shop. And we don't want that, do we?'

'No,' said Raphael warily. 'We definitely don't want that.'

'So if I could put my brain to work and ensure that the letters stopped,' said Jemma, 'that would be a good thing, wouldn't it?' She paused, sprayed more polish, and worked on.

Folio stretched out a foreleg and began to wash it. Raphael tickled his tummy.

The light outside grew a little brighter and a sunbeam shone golden light on the counter, illuminating the rich red grain.

'And it would keep me busy,' said Jemma. 'Along with restocking the shelves, and serving the customers, and keeping the shop tidy, of course.'

'Of course,' agreed Raphael. 'I must admit that it isn't a pleasant situation, and if we could see them off that would be wonderful.'

'I'm not promising anything,' said Jemma, applying

slightly more pressure to the shop counter. 'It could be too difficult for me to solve. But I'll try.'

'That would be very kind of you,' said Raphael. Folio rumbled out a purr.

'OK, then,' said Jemma, addressing the counter. 'I'll see what I can do.' It took all her strength not to punch the air, or exclaim 'Yes! Did it!', or to dismiss the counter with a final brisk rub. Somehow she managed it, polishing the whole counter with the same careful attention. She allowed herself one quiet round of applause when she went to put the polish away, and that was all.

When she came back in, Raphael regarded her curiously. 'How do you think you'll go about it?' he asked.

'I'm not exactly sure,' said Jemma, grinning inwardly. 'Let me have a think, and maybe I can get started after lunch.'

'Oh. Very well,' said Raphael, and returned to his newspaper.

It's working, thought Jemma. *My plan is actually working*. She felt pleasingly smug that she had managed to get round Raphael, Folio, *and* the shop with her clever side-swerve. She went to the stockroom and brought out another box, which yielded a stack of Miss Marple novels and a complete set of Sherlock Holmes. *The game is afoot*, she thought, and she couldn't stop herself from smiling.

Chapter 11

Jemma had said she would start her investigation after lunch; however, in reality she planned to begin a little earlier. 'Is it all right if I pop out for a sandwich?' she asked, at around twelve o'clock. 'If I go now, I can probably miss the rush.'

Raphael looked up from *Devil in a Blue Dress*. 'Yes, of course,' he said. 'I'll nip out when you get back.'

'I won't be too long,' said Jemma, edging towards the door. 'See you later.'

Her first stop was at Rolando's. Despite going early there was still a queue, and she had to wait a few minutes to place her order. However, this gave her time to watch the barista, who was a graceful young man with rich brown skin. 'It's my first time in here,' she remarked, when her turn came. Unfortunately the roar of the coffee machine completely drowned her out.

'I'm sorry, what was that?' Could he be Rolando? Surely he was too young. She peered at the name badge on his chest: *Carl*.

'I said this is my first time,' she shouted. All the noise stopped part-way through her announcement, and someone giggled. 'In here, I mean,' she said, conscious that her cheeks were burning. 'I've just started working in Burns Books. Um, can I have a cappuccino, please?'

'Coming up,' said the barista. He turned away, poured milk into a metal jug and began frothing it. At the same time, he made an espresso. Jemma kept her eyes on his shoulder blades.

'Have you been into the bookshop?' she asked.

'Not yet, no,' said the barista. 'I haven't worked here long.' He poured milk into the cup and dusted the top with cocoa powder. 'There you go.'

'Maybe you could drop in some time,' said Jemma, determined to salvage something from her failed mission. 'We've got lots of books.'

Carl looked slightly puzzled. 'Yes, I suppose you would have.'

'I'm Jemma, by the way,' said Jemma, and felt the person behind her in the queue shuffle closer. She sighed, and moved to the till to pay for her drink. While the cappuccino would no doubt be lovely, she didn't think the intelligence she had received was a fair swap for three pounds. *Never mind*, she thought, *I have a contact.*

Her next port of call was the mini-market. 'Plenty of egg mayo,' called Nafisa.

'I might have a change today,' said Jemma. 'What

would you recommend?'

Nafisa came out from behind the counter and scrutinised the selection of sandwiches and wraps. Her nose wrinkled. 'Home cooking,' she said.

'I work in Burns Books,' said Jemma, apropos of nothing.

Nafisa laughed. 'For now,' she said.

Jemma frowned. 'What do you mean?'

Nafisa's dark eyes sparkled. 'That shop's had more assistants than a bad magician.'

Jemma continued to regard the display, her heart thumping. 'Why do you think that is?' she asked, as casually as she knew how.

'No idea,' said Nafisa. 'I don't know what he does with them.'

'Maybe they don't get on,' said Jemma. After some thought, she selected tuna and cucumber on wholemeal bread.

Nafisa shrugged. 'Maybe. He's always perfectly polite when he comes in here. He looks a bit down if I haven't got his teabags in, but he's never rude. Are you taking that?' She stretched out her hand for the sandwich. 'Anything else?'

On an impulse, Jemma moved to the biscuit selection. 'And these,' she said, picking up a packet of custard creams. She wasn't entirely sure what biscuits Raphael liked, but she felt you couldn't go wrong with a custard cream.

'OK, that's two pounds ten,' said Nafisa. She rang up the items, and Jemma paid with her phone. 'Good luck!'

She flashed a broad grin at Jemma, then went back to pricing up a tray of tinned tomatoes.

Jemma considered trying more shops in the parade; but her hands were full, and she was conscious that she had already been out for twenty minutes. *Besides*, she thought, *I must write all this up while it's fresh in my mind.*

She returned to the shop, and was surprised to find Raphael dealing with a customer. A customer he knew, from his level of alertness. He was a tall, stooped man with a fierce white moustache, wearing baggy corduroy trousers of indeterminate colour, a burnt-orange waistcoat, and a cheesecloth shirt. 'So if you happen to have that elusive third volume, Raphael, I'll give you a good price for it.'

A crafty gleam came into Raphael's eye. 'What's a good price, Brian?'

Brian drew himself up and gazed at the cash register, then at Raphael. 'We've done a lot of business together, Raphael,' he said briskly. 'And as we're in the same trade, I know there's no cheating you. So I'll err on the side of generosity and say fifty.'

Raphael straightened up too, so that he was slightly taller than Brian. 'You'll lose the sale without that volume,' he said. 'I can let you have it for eighty.'

Brian laughed. 'What use is one volume to you? I'm doing you a favour by taking it off your hands. If you don't grab this opportunity, you'll probably still have that book in twenty years' time.' He paused. 'I'll go up to sixty, then.'

'If I don't grab this opportunity,' said Raphael, his words dripping with sarcasm, 'I'm prepared to wait.

Seventy-five, and not a penny less.'

The two men's eyes met. They stared at each other for perhaps a minute and a half before Brian's gaze dropped to the shop counter. 'I'll remember this next time you need a favour,' he said. 'Go on, show me the book. I'll pay your price if it's in good condition. Otherwise, you can whistle.'

'Jemma, would you mind fetching the book for me?' said Raphael, still looking at Brian. 'Volume three of Geeling's *Metaphysical Studies*. You'll find it in the Science section, in the middle of the top row.'

'You've got it on display?' Jemma heard Brian say as she retreated towards the back of the shop. She fetched the ladder, climbed up, and found a leather-bound chestnut-brown book with its title stamped in gold. She slid it out carefully, descended the ladder, and hurried to lay it on the counter.

'Hmmm,' said Brian, bending over the book until his nose nearly touched it. 'May I?' He motioned with a hand towards the cover.

'Be my guest,' said Raphael, all affability.

Brian opened the book in a few different places, letting the leaves slip through his fingers. The volume was closely printed in two columns, with several intricate diagrams.

'Righto,' he said, closing the book. He reached into his waistcoat pocket and extracted a slim wallet. 'I suppose you're still a troglodyte when it comes to money.' He counted out four twenties. 'Got a fiver?'

Raphael opened the till and handed him a five-pound note without looking down. 'Need a receipt?'

'If you don't mind,' said Brian. 'Always helpful to keep

things square.'

Raphael took a receipt book from the drawer and filled in the details. Jemma watched the intricate loops and swirls of his elegant hand, and wondered where on earth he had learnt to write like that. 'There you are,' he said, handing it over. 'Pleasure doing business with you, Brian. Would you like a bag?'

'I think I can manage,' Brian said heavily. He tucked the book under his arm, nodded to them both, and left the shop.

Jemma exhaled, then took the lid off her cappuccino. It was still fairly warm. 'Who was he?' she asked.

'That was Brian,' said Raphael. 'Weren't you listening?'

'Well, yes,' said Jemma, 'but he obviously wasn't a normal customer.'

'I'm not sure we have such a thing as a normal customer,' said Raphael. 'He's a bookseller. Antiquarian.'

'Oh, right,' said Jemma. 'But we're not, are we?'

'Good grief, no,' said Raphael, and laughed as if the very idea were absurd.

Jemma took another sip of her cappuccino, then regarded him over the top of her disposable cup with what she felt to be a steely gaze. 'Then how did he know to come here?' she said, setting her drink down with an unimpressive tap on the counter. 'How did he know you might have the book he wanted?'

'Word gets around,' said Raphael. 'Besides, Brian and I go back a long way.'

'Oh.' Jemma imagined Brian perhaps twenty-five years ago, with a slightly less ferocious moustache and newer corduroys, showing Raphael the ropes of the bookselling business. 'Did he teach you everything you know?' she asked, with a smile.

'Oh no, I was here first,' said Raphael. 'Are those biscuits?' He pointed at the custard creams.

'Yes, they are,' said Jemma. 'Why don't you open them?'

Raphael's hand stretched towards the packet, then hesitated. 'Actually, I might go for my lunch,' he said, eyeing Jemma's tuna sandwich with curiosity. 'Is that all right? It's been quiet, Brian's been the only customer since you went out.'

'That's absolutely fine,' said Jemma, though she would have liked to continue their conversation about Brian, and perhaps extend it to other booksellers with whom he had a similar relationship. Had they been hostile towards each other? Not really. And friendly wasn't right either, although they had seemed reasonably cordial. Ambivalent, perhaps? Then she remembered watching two stags fight on a wildlife program. This hadn't been anything like as alarming, but she had a definite sense they were vying for the upper hand. While Raphael had got it this time, she suspected Brian would bear that in mind for the next encounter. *I must write all this down*, she thought.

She didn't have long to wait, for Raphael was already buttoning his jacket. 'You'll be fine, won't you?' he said, which Jemma took to be his way of telling her that it would be a long lunch. 'Negotiating with Brian does take it out of me, rather.'

'You surprised me,' said Jemma. 'I didn't think you'd

be so . . . businesslike.' She had almost said *ruthless*.

'I let him off lightly,' said Raphael. 'That book is easily worth a hundred pounds, and Brian knows it.'

'Is that because it's old and rare?' asked Jemma.

Raphael's eyes gleamed, but he hesitated before replying. 'Yes, it's old and reasonably rare,' he said. 'And of course when someone needs a book to complete their set, that allows you to add a bit on. Anyway, I'd better go.' He strode to the door and left without looking back.

Jemma watched him hurry past the window, and shrugged. Then she opened her bag and pulled out the notebook and pen she had packed that morning. She opened it at the first page, wrote *Investigation*, and underlined it. Then she wrote the date, and *Initial Findings*.

- *Visited Rolando's. Spoke to Carl, barista. Doesn't know R, hasn't been in the shop, is new. Cappuccino very nice. Also Carl.*
- *Called in at mini-market for sandwich and biscuits. Nafisa says R's assistants don't stay long, but he's always polite.*
- *Returned to find antiquarian bookseller Brian and R negotiating over book. R was ruthless. Sounds as if this behaviour is long-standing. Could letters come from angry bookseller who doesn't like R's methods?*

Jemma underlined the last sentence, feeling pleased with herself. Her stomach rumbled. *Detective work does make one rather hungry.* She peeled the film back from the

84

sandwich box, smiling in anticipation, lifted a sandwich out, and took a large bite. Then she grimaced as her palate adjusted to dry tuna, slimy cucumber, and damp, thin bread. She looked at her notebook and added another sentence: *Don't buy the tuna and cucumber sandwich again.* However relevant or otherwise Nafisa's other observations had been, perhaps she was right about home cooking.

Chapter 12

The afternoon passed quickly. Jemma was kept busy dealing with customers in the shop. They seemed more demanding than usual; maybe Brian had left some sort of pernickety residue behind which had influenced them.

Raphael, as predicted, had taken an extremely long lunch break indeed, returning to the shop at about two thirty. Jemma wondered how on earth he had managed before she came along. Had he been tied to the shop? If anything, she suspected he had merely turned the shop sign from open to closed, and kept the hours he currently did.

When he returned, he did lend a hand with the customers, though. Jemma hurried back and forth, fetching books and laying them on the counter for inspection, and replenishing the stock whenever she got a minute. She noted that the boxes she opened contained more Golden Age crime, Brother Cadfael novels, and some slightly dogeared Nancy Drew books. *Don't lose sight of your mission, Jemma*, she told herself, as she unpacked yet another box.

In the end they didn't close the shop until a quarter past five, and then there was cashing-up to be done, accompanied by a cup of tea, as there had not been time to make a brew since lunch. 'Look at the time,' said Raphael, as he picked up bundles of notes and bank bags full of coins, ready for the safe. 'At this rate I shall have to consider paying overtime.'

'Oh, don't worry about it,' said Jemma, without thinking. 'I used to work much later in my last job. I'll take a long lunch one day, or come in later.'

Raphael eyed her doubtfully. 'If you're sure,' he said. 'But get yourself off home now, and I'll see you tomorrow.'

Jemma slung her bag over her shoulder, and left. She had intended to visit more shops in the parade, but most were closed. There was the takeaway, but she didn't want to risk temptation, and the only other one still open was an estate agent called Ransome's, whose window bore the slogan *NO ONE DOES IT CHEAPER!* Jemma glanced at the properties on display; lots of flats to rent, and shops too.

A young man in a shiny suit came out of the shop and accosted her. 'What sort of thing are you looking for?'

'Oh, I'm not, not really,' said Jemma. *Then again,* she thought, *it might be worth seeing if there are any nice flats in the area.* Perhaps she could cut out the tube and save money.

'Come on, people are always after something,' said the man.

'Well, I could look, I suppose,' said Jemma. 'I work in the bookshop. Burns Books.'

The young man frowned. 'Burns Books, you say?'

'I know, it's a funny name,' said Jemma. 'I've just started there, and I'm trying to find out a little more about the neighbourhood.'

'Ah, property around here, you see, it looks nice – or some of it does – but you want to watch out,' said the man, licking his lips. 'Unfortunately, being in a nice bit of London doesn't always count for much.'

'Really?' said Jemma. 'What about location, location, location?'

'You don't want to listen to that rubbish,' said the man gloomily. 'They don't know what it's like at the sharp end. A shop with an upstairs and everything, you'd think it would be worth a tidy packet, wouldn't you? But given the state of it, and that it's in the wrong part of Charing Cross Road, well, you'd have to pay me to take it off your hands.'

Jemma frowned. 'I was actually wondering about flats for rent nearby,' she said.

'Oh, right,' said the young man, without much more enthusiasm. 'Bit dangerous at night. Wouldn't recommend this area for a young lady.'

Once Jemma had insisted that she could look after herself, stalked into the estate agent's, and demanded to be shown some flats, the young man brought her a selection of five depressing properties, all smaller and more expensive than the studio flat she currently inhabited. 'I see what you mean,' said Jemma. 'Thank you for your time.'

'Been a pleasure,' said the young man, shuffling the information sheets into a pile.

It was half past six by the time Jemma got home. She dropped her bag on the sofa and considered going back out for a takeaway, or even breaking her own rule and getting one delivered. *No*, she told herself. *You've done so well. Don't spoil it now*. She perused the recipe book, and decided that pasta primavera would be healthy yet also comforting. It had been a long day. She took the book to the kitchenette, and began assembling ingredients.

As she chopped, on the worktop which was perhaps four inches higher than she would have liked it, she idly thought that it was a shame all the flats near Charing Cross Road had been so disappointing. It came to something when even an estate agent couldn't recommend anything.

Then her knife was arrested, mid-chop. The estate agent had said Raphael's shop wasn't worth a great deal. That meant whoever had written the letters hadn't done it because they wanted to get their hands on the shop. Jemma put her knife down and ran to fetch her notebook. *Getting hold of shop not a motive*, she scribbled. *Not worth a lot. Estate agent said wrong part of Charing Cross Road*. She thought for a moment, then added: *Perhaps R aware of this and therefore unwilling to invest money or time in shop?*

She was considering this nugget of information when her phone rang. The display said *Em*.

'Hi, Jemma,' said Em. 'Fancy meeting up for a drink? We're heading to the Marquis in a minute.'

Jemma looked at the half-chopped vegetables in front of her. 'Thanks, Em, but I've only just got in. We closed late, you see.'

'You stayed late?' said Em, with an odd note in her voice. 'I hope you're getting overtime for that.'

Jemma laughed. 'I'll take a long lunch tomorrow. Actually, no, Wednesdays tend to be busy.'

Em huffed out a sigh, and Jemma could imagine her rolling her eyes. 'Don't let the owner take advantage of you, Jemma. Before you know where you are you'll be working through your lunch hour and staying late, and for what?' She paused, and when she spoke again her voice was bright. 'Anyway, that doesn't stop you coming for a quick one, does it?'

Jemma eyed her notebook. 'I've got something to do after I've had dinner. But I can come out another time,' she added hurriedly.

Another pause. 'Jemma, you're a sweet person, and very trusting, and I love that about you,' said Em. 'But I have to admit that I think this bookshop job is a bad move. I bet you're working for almost nothing and wearing yourself into the ground.'

'I like it,' Jemma began, but Em wasn't finished.

'I mean, are you using your skills? Really? You'll end up just as unappreciated as you were before. I hate to say it, but Phoebe walked all over you, and this bookshop person will do exactly the same thing if you're not careful. Now I'm heading out, and if you have any sense you'll join me. I hope I'll see you later.' And the call ended.

Jemma stared at her phone. It was completely unlike

Em to get annoyed. She looked at the vegetables, then at her notebook, then her watch. It was getting on for seven. Slowly, she resumed chopping, but Em's words made her feel a little queasy. *Is Raphael taking advantage of me?* she thought. *After all, he won't let me do what I'm good at, and now I'm running around investigating. Mostly in my own time.*

'Ow!' She looked down; she had nicked her thumb with the knife. 'For heaven's sake!' She threw the knife down in disgust, washed her hands at the sink, and went in search of a plaster. Then she scooped the vegetables into a container, slammed it into the fridge, found the takeaway menu, and rang for a pizza. She didn't trust herself to go for a drink with Em; she suspected that if she did, she would end up rambling loudly and incoherently, and possibly being put into a taxi. Instead, she went to the wine rack and opened a bottle of Chilean red.

***

'Morning,' said Raphael, when Jemma arrived at the shop the next morning. 'Well, more or less.'

'Morning,' muttered Jemma. *I'm clearly out of practice*, she thought. Last night's wine and pepperoni pizza were proving uneasy bedfellows. To make it worse, the bright morning light pierced her brain like a laser. She wished she had been able to find her sunglasses, but even after standing under the shower for twenty minutes, getting dressed and out of the flat had taken all her capability.

'Tea?' said Raphael, in an irritatingly jaunty voice. 'I mean, I've had a cup already, but I can always put the kettle on again.'

'Coffee. Black,' said Jemma. 'I'll do it.' She went into the back room, where at least there were no windows to torture her, and flicked the kettle on. While she waited she leaned on the worktop, her head in her hands. She tried to remember exactly what Em had said, but it was jumbled up in a resentful haze. Maybe Raphael was taking advantage of her. He'd said himself that she could take the time back, and now he was teasing her about it. *Em's right, I'm being played for a fool,* Jemma thought bitterly, and put two heaped teaspoons of coffee into her mug.

She heard a small, low-pitched meow, and Folio jumped onto the worktop, his tail a question mark. 'You're not supposed to be on there,' said Jemma, scooping him up and setting him on the floor.

Folio purred, rubbed his head against her shin, and gazed up at her with amber eyes.

'I'm not cross with you,' she said, rather crossly. 'I'm cross with him, and – and *things.*'

'Would you like some toast?' called Raphael. 'You look a bit, um, hungry.'

Typical, thought Jemma, as she dropped two slices of white into the toaster and rammed the catch down. *He's worked out that I'm on to him, and he's buttering me up.*

But there was no denying that after half a mug of black coffee and a slice of toast, Jemma felt considerably better. By the time she went back into the shop the sun had had the decency to retreat behind a cloud, which made things much more bearable.

'I was a bit later than I intended,' said Jemma. 'Sorry.'

'That's quite all right,' said Raphael. 'I'm sure you've

worked extra, anyway. Now, do you mind if I nip out for twenty minutes or so?'

Here we go, thought Jemma.

Raphael gestured to a small stack of books on the counter. 'I had a call earlier from an acquaintance of mine who owns a shop down the road. He needs a few books to complete an order, and as it happens, I've got them. He's single-handed and can't leave the shop, so I said I'd pop round with them when I could get away.'

Jemma felt heat creeping up her neck. 'Oh, absolutely,' she said. 'Sorry I kept you waiting.'

'No need to apologise,' said Raphael. 'Are you sure you can manage?' He did actually appear concerned.

'I'm fine,' said Jemma. 'Had a glass of wine too many last night,' she confessed.

Raphael laughed. 'Oh, we've all done that. I'll be as quick as I can.'

Once he had gone Jemma looked around the shop for things to do, but everything appeared in good order. There weren't obvious gaps on the shelves, the till had a float, and Raphael had replaced their stock of paper bags. *I could sit and read.* She opened her bag, pulled out the copy of *Anna Karenina* which had been there for some time, then put it back and found *Lucy Sullivan Is Getting Married* instead. *I bet a customer will come in before I finish the first page*, she thought, and sat in the armchair. Folio settled next to her, his furry bulk pressing against her elbow.

Jemma was about thirty pages in when the shop bell rang. She sighed, and looked up.

'Um, hello?' said a nervous youth in an army-surplus coat, holding a sheet of paper covered in scribble. 'I've got a reading list for my dissertation topic, and I wondered if you had any of the books.'

Jemma hunted for a bookmark, and finding none, used a paper bag instead. 'I can check,' she said, holding her hand out for the list.

Fifteen minutes later her customer, balancing a teetering pile of books, headed for the door. 'Oh, you've got a letter,' he said. 'I'd pick it up, but…'

Jemma saw a square, pale-blue envelope face down on the doormat. 'I'll get it in a minute,' she said, and went to hold the door open for him.

When he had gone, she didn't pick the envelope up immediately. *It's nothing like the first one. It's probably a card.* On turning it over, she saw that the envelope was addressed to Burns Books in neat, forward-slanting writing. It was unstamped.

It won't be another anonymous letter. And if it is, I can analyse it properly. It won't be like last time, when Raphael took the note away before I'd had a chance to look at it. Before she could change her mind, she ripped it open.

Inside was a piece of pale-blue notepaper, folded in half, but Jemma could feel unevenness through the paper. She took a deep breath, and opened it out.

kEEp YOuR nOSe OuT, uNdERLiNg, oR wE'll cOmE fOR yOu TOo

94

Chapter 13

Jemma felt her knees wobble. She hurried to the armchair and sat down, still staring at the note. She was conscious of a strangeness about the air, as if a thunderstorm approached.

Who's sending these? And why are they coming after me?

Because they know you want to track them down. They're scared of you.

Jemma closed her eyes and visualised Raphael saying 'empty threats'. She repeated the words like a mantra, and as she did so the oppressive atmosphere seemed to lift. She smelt vanilla, and cinnamon, though she couldn't work out where it was coming from. Surely not the note? She sniffed it, but it smelt of paper, and faintly of glue.

The shop bell jangled and she looked up, guiltily. Raphael came through the door smiling, a paper bag in his hand. 'Most satisfactory,' he announced. 'I got cinnamon rolls from Rolando's to celebrate. Is it too early for elevenses, do you think?' Then he took in her expression. 'What's wrong, Jemma?'

Jemma looked at the note in her hands. 'The anonymous letter-writer strikes again,' she said, trying to keep her voice light.

'Oh no, not again.' Raphael walked over and held his hand out for the letter. 'Don't pay any attention. Here, I'll get rid of it.'

'No, I'll do it,' said Jemma, screwing the letter up into a ball. 'And I'll make tea to go with the cinnamon rolls.'

'Oh yes, good idea,' said Raphael, but he still seemed worried. 'Are you sure you're all right?'

'Yes, fine,' said Jemma, already on her way to the back room. 'All in a day's work. We had a customer while you were out. He bought lots of music theory books.'

'Oh good,' said Raphael. 'I did wonder, when I unpacked that box, how long we'd have them for. Not as long as I thought.'

In the back room, Jemma smoothed out the letter and replaced it in its envelope. *No one threatens me*, she thought, grimly. *The more they try to put me off, the more determined I am to catch them.*

When she took the tea through, Raphael was ensconced in the armchair. 'So which books did you take round to your colleague?' she asked.

'Works about the Knights Templar,' said Raphael. 'A historian friend of his is working on a new book, and looking for research materials.'

'The Knights Templar?' asked Jemma. 'Who or what are they?'

Raphael's eye-roll was subtle, but still discernible. 'I'd tell you to go and read a book about them, Jemma,' he said. 'But at the moment, we don't have any. Ah, tea. Thank you.' He took a sip, then set his cup down with a sigh of pleasure. 'Jemma, I've been thinking. Maybe you shouldn't seek out this letter-writing chump. Perhaps you're right, and it is a police matter.'

'But I thought you didn't want the police round here asking questions?' said Jemma. Her cup trembled in her hand, and she put it on the counter. Suddenly she felt as if she were at the top of a mountain; it was hard to breathe. 'Like you said, it's a load of silly notes.'

'I know,' said Raphael. 'But just because something's silly, that doesn't mean it can't be dangerous. Look at bungee jumping.'

'What has bungee jumping got to do with anything?' said Jemma. 'The police will probably laugh at you, anyway. I don't think we should get the police involved, not at all.'

'Is that your honest opinion?' said Raphael, frowning.

'Yes,' said Jemma. 'I think we should get on with the day-to-day business of running the shop and ignore it, like you said.' As she said it, her lightheadedness began to fade.

'Yes, I did say that, didn't I?' Folio jumped on Raphael's lap, purred, and butted his head against Raphael's hand. 'And the shop does take a fair bit of running. Particularly now that we're so busy.'

As if they had heard this, two women came in. 'My,

what a lovely little bookshop!' exclaimed the shorter one, in a southern American accent. 'I simply must have a look around!'

Twenty minutes later, they left. The enthusiastic woman had bought nothing, but her silent companion had bought all the Charlaine Harris in stock. 'I'll go and get more books,' said Jemma, wondering what a random box selection would turn up.

'Don't forget your cinnamon roll,' said Raphael. 'They're very good.'

'I'll have it when I've restocked,' said Jemma. It did look tempting; but she felt she needed a breathing space more than sugar.

Jemma took her time in the stockroom, wandering down the aisles and trailing her hand along the boxes. *I'll have to do this undercover*, she thought. *Raphael can't catch me with the note. I'll go out for lunch, and see what I can accomplish.* She could feel her heart thumping, and took a few deep breaths before selecting a box and going back to the main shop. When she opened it, she found that the box was full of Hercule Poirot mysteries, all vintage.

'Those will do well,' said Raphael. 'There are a lot of Agatha fans and collectors out there.'

'Yes, there are,' Jemma replied, smiling. She was sure that there were; but she was happier that her choice of box appeared to indicate that she was doing the right thing. It was almost as if the shop approved, although of course that was ridiculous.

Raphael went for his lunch first, and as soon as he was safely away, Jemma spread the note on the shop counter and retrieved her notebook. She wrote the date, then *New Development.*

A second note arrived between 9.30 and around 10.15. Note apparently for me. She copied it out, including the capital letters. *Sender addressed me as 'underling' so we can assume they don't know my name.* She pursed her lips, and read what she had written. *Or do they?*

She examined the note. *The envelope and the paper don't match*, she wrote. *The envelope is a slightly different blue, and the wrong size for the notepaper. The previous note was on standard A4 paper, and was in a long white envelope. It looked like office stationery, while this looks like an envelope from a greetings card, and notepaper from a pad.* She held it up to the light, peered at it, and noted: *Basildon Bond.*

Next she examined the text. *The note is composed of letters cut from newspapers and/or magazines.* On impulse, she fetched Raphael's newspaper and studied the headlines. The letters looked similar, but not exactly the same. She sighed, and picked up her pen again.

At lunchtime, check a selection of publications for a match.

She took a picture of the note with her phone, focusing as closely as she could on the letters, then put it in her bag. *It would be just my luck for Raphael to walk in on me at the mini-market*, she thought. *This way I can lock my phone, and he'll never know.*

The time dragged until Raphael returned. Jemma made a list of all the shops in the parade, then all the people who might bear a grudge against Raphael. This included rival bookshop owners, booksellers with whom he had driven a hard bargain, former assistants (she wrote '*who are still alive*' next to this entry), and Mr Tennant from the Retail Association. However you looked at it, it really wasn't a detailed list. *I must find out more about him.* She unlocked her phone and typed *Raphael Burns* into Google.

Nothing came up; or at least, nothing that was related to Raphael. She tried *Raphael Burns bookseller*, and got the same result. 'That's weird,' she said. 'How can there be nothing on the internet about someone?' She Googled her own name for comparison and three pages of information came up, including her neglected Twitter feed, her Instagram, which was mainly photos of beverages, and her company profile. *They haven't even bothered to delete me*, she thought, and blinked.

Then she typed in *Burns Books Charing Cross Road*. The first entry was from TripAdvisor: *Read 54 unbiased reviews of Burns Books*. Remembering the article she had read, Jemma held her breath as she clicked the link.

It was even worse than she had thought. The shop had an average rating of 1.5.

I had to have a tetanus jab after the shop cat attacked me.

I couldn't pay for my book for 15 minutes because the owner was building a house of cards on the counter.

I shall never set foot in this bookshop again. I'd like to

100

tell you why, but children might read this.

'Oh dear,' murmured Jemma. At the bottom of her list of people she added: *Almost anyone who has visited the shop. See TripAdvisor for more details.* 'Careful what you wish for, Jemma,' she said to herself. 'You wanted more suspects, and now you have plenty.'

Raphael came in, and Jemma pretended to be reading the newspaper. 'Nice and quiet, then?' he asked.

'Yes, pretty much,' Jemma replied. 'I'll head out for my lunch, if that's OK.'

'Yes, go ahead,' said Raphael, walking to the crime shelves and selecting *Murder On The Orient Express.*

'Good choice,' said Jemma. She frowned. What if – what if a group of disgruntled customers were taking it upon themselves to drive Raphael out of business?

Don't be daft, she told herself. *It would make much more sense for them to go to a different bookshop. And that would be a lot less trouble.* She got her jacket, and set off for the mini-market. *Time for more research.* But even in the half a minute that it took her to get there, her other internet discovery – or rather, lack of discovery – nagged at her. *How is it possible for a normal human being to have absolutely no presence on social media whatsoever?*

You shouldn't be surprised, she told herself. *He doesn't even have a card machine in the shop. Modern technology's completely beyond him.* She pushed open the door of the mini-market with a pleasing sense of superiority. *Time for me to drag him into the modern world.*

Chapter 14

'Afternoon,' said Nafisa as Jemma entered the shop. 'Will you be browsing our sandwich selection again today?'

'I think I'll stick to egg mayo,' said Jemma. She got a sandwich from the cabinet, and after some thought, added a can of Diet Coke and a Twix. She put those on the counter, then went to the newspaper section and took out her phone. Opening the picture, she compared the typefaces on the photo with those in front of her.

'I suppose at least you're not reading them,' said Nafisa. 'What are you doing?'

'I'm, er, looking for something,' said Jemma.

'I can see that,' Nafisa replied. Shaking her head, she carried on reading her magazine.

Jemma glanced across, and her eye snagged on the headline. 'What magazine is that, please?'

'*Take a Break*,' said Nafisa.

'Right. Thanks,' said Jemma, and added a *Take a Break* to the pile. Then she peered at her phone again, and put a *Daily Mail* on top of it. She scanned the other newspapers and magazines, but nothing was quite right. 'That'll do,' she said.

Nafisa rang up her purchases. 'Slow day today?' she asked.

'Oh no, Raphael says it's much busier since I've come,' said Jemma. 'I'm getting these for, um, later.'

'No need to explain to me,' said Nafisa, laughing.

She passed the card machine over and Jemma touched her phone to it. 'How much do these cost?' she asked, pointing at it.

'Oh, not much,' said Nafisa. 'Got this one a few years ago, but now you can pick up a card reader for about twenty quid if you shop around.'

'That's good to know,' said Jemma. 'I'm thinking of setting the bookshop up to take electronic payments.'

'Really?' Nafisa's eyes were as round and bright as new pennies. She snorted. 'Good luck with that.'

Jemma looked at her curiously. 'Why do you say that?'

'Oh, no reason,' said Nafisa, waving a casual hand. 'He just doesn't seem the type. I mean, he wears those waistcoats.'

'Lots of people wear waistcoats,' said Jemma.

'Waistcoats, yes,' said Nafisa. 'But not those waistcoats.' She nodded with an air of ineffable wisdom.

'Right, well, thanks,' said Jemma, gathering up her purchases. 'See you tomorrow, I guess.'

'See you tomorrow,' said Nafisa, already absorbed in

her magazine.

Jemma considered calling in at a few more shops to try and glean more information about Raphael, but she had already used ten minutes of her lunch hour. So she decamped to the Phoenix Garden, found a bench in the sunshine, and spread out her picnic, publications, and the fateful letter.

She ate half her sandwich without realising, so intent was she on matching the letters in her note. *Take a Break*, as it turned out, was a valuable source of different typographical styles and colours. Fifteen minutes later, Jemma had identified perhaps two-thirds of the letters. Then she studied the *Daily Mail*, which was particularly useful for the capitals.

Jemma ate the second half of her sandwich while considering the last two unidentified letters: a Y with a curious flourish on its right-hand arm, and an intricate g whose lower loop was narrow and slanted. Both were black, on a cream background, and Jemma didn't recall seeing anything like them in either a magazine or a newspaper.

'Still pretty good work, though,' she said to herself. She unwrapped her Twix and ate half before realising that she was already full. *I'll save the other half for the tube*, she thought, and put it back in its wrapper. 'Back to it, I suppose,' she said, brushing her hands together, and headed towards the bustle of Charing Cross Road.

But as she came to the parade of shops in which Burns Books was located, she hesitated. Was it worth another look in the mini-market to track down the elusive last two letters? Could she even, perhaps, show the letters to Nafisa – in close-up, of course – and see if she recognised them? After all, she handled dozens of publications every day. Surely the chances were good.

'Is it tomorrow already?' said Nafisa as Jemma hurried in. Jemma detected distinct testiness in Nafisa's tone. Now was clearly not a good time for special requests.

'It's OK,' she said, edging towards the door, but scanning the magazine shelves as she did so. 'To be honest, I've forgotten what I came in for.'

'At your age? That's bad,' said Nafisa. 'Are you going back to the shop?'

'Yes, that's right,' said Jemma. She reached for the door handle.

'In that case, can you tell Raphael that his *Bookseller's Companion* has come in? I'd give it to you to pass on, but if I do he'll never remember to pay me.' She reached under the counter and brought out an odd-looking publication, printed on cream-coloured paper with bold black typography.

Jemma stared at it. 'I can take that for him,' she said. 'Don't worry, I'll pay you.' She fumbled for her phone and held it to the card machine, her eyes never leaving the magazine in Nafisa's hand.

Nafisa laughed. 'Are you going to read it before you give it to him? You're keen.'

'Yes I am, rather,' said Jemma. 'I'd better get back. Bye, Nafisa.'

But Jemma did not return to the bookshop. She stood outside the mini-market and leafed through the magazine until she had found the letters she wanted, in articles headed *Your Book Care Tips* and *Reading Recommendations: Friend or Foe*? Only then did she allow anger to wash over her.

'Him all along!' she said, her voice as bitter as strong black coffee. She imagined Raphael upstairs in his flat, which was probably an absolute tip filled with unwashed mugs and smelling of cat. He would lounge on a battered old chesterfield sofa which had probably been worth a lot of money before he mistreated it, and which would have horsehair leaking from the cushions. A pot of paste and a pile of old magazines would sit on the stained low table in front of him, and he'd arrange the letters on a sheet of paper and chuckle to himself at how stupid she was.

'I should have realised,' she muttered. 'No wonder he was always out when the letters came. He was the one delivering them! All this to stop me from turning that shop around!'

Jemma had worked herself up into a storm of fury by the time she pushed open the door of Burns Books. Luckily for Raphael, he was actually dealing with a customer, and while Jemma was tempted to denounce him then and there, she told herself that she was far too professional to do that sort of thing.

At length the customer departed, clutching a copy of *The Accused*. The moment the door closed behind him, Jemma stalked over and threw the *Bookseller's Companion* onto the counter. 'I know what you've been doing,' she said.

Raphael immediately looked very guilty indeed. 'Oh,'

he said. He bit his bottom lip. 'Do you?'

'Yes,' said Jemma, 'I do.'

'Oh dear,' said Raphael. He grimaced. 'That's awkward.'

'Yes, it is,' snapped Jemma. 'Maybe I should be flattered that you went to so much trouble to stop me doing my job.'

Raphael frowned. 'Your job?'

'Yes, my job,' spat Jemma. 'Or what should be my job; dragging this bookshop into the twenty-first century and making it a going concern instead of the shambles it currently is. Look at it!' She swept a hand round the interior, which appeared particularly grey and dismal. 'Nothing on the walls, no extras or accessories for customers to buy, no recommendations, nowhere for customers to sit except an armchair which you and that cat hog all the time.' One of the lights above Jemma's head flickered, buzzed, and went out, but she kept going. 'I've read the reviews on TripAdvisor. I know what people are saying about this shop. You ought to be grateful that I work here at all. And now you've pulled a stunt like this!'

She took a breath and focused on Raphael, who seemed utterly bemused. 'Jemma, I have absolutely no idea what you mean,' he said.

'This shop is a pigsty!' she cried. 'Most of your customers hate you! And instead of doing anything about it, you spend your time faking stupid anonymous letters to distract me!'

'Me?' said Raphael. 'You think I sent them?'

'You did it all right,' said Jemma. She took the letter

107

out of her bag, unfolded it, and stabbed an accusing finger at the Y and the g. 'Those letters come from this magazine, and I know Nafisa orders it in for you, because she told me. Letters from this, and the *Daily Mail*, and *Take a Break*, all of which you can buy from her. All your flannel about business ecosystems and balance is just that; a load of old flannel. You can't face the fact that you, Raphael Burns, are a failure, and so is this crappy excuse for a bookshop.' The door rattled, and cold air blasted Jemma's ankles. 'You've got a motive and plenty of opportunity, and all the evidence points to you.' She folded her arms and glared at him. 'So as far as I'm concerned, it's up to you to prove me wrong.'

Chapter 15

'I admit that it doesn't look good,' said Raphael. 'But it really wasn't me.'

'Prove it,' said Jemma.

Folio jumped onto the counter and yowled at her, but she ignored him. 'It stinks, and you know it.'

'I'm rather hurt that you'd think such a thing of me,' said Raphael. 'I mean, as if I'd read the *Daily Mail.*'

Jemma's mouth twitched in spite of herself. Then she banged the counter with her fist. 'It isn't funny! How dare you send me off on a wild-goose chase! But the joke's on you, Raphael. I could have made something of the shop, if you'd let me, but why should I bother now?'

'The shop,' said Raphael, with dignity, 'is already something, thank you very much.'

'Yes, it is,' sneered Jemma. 'It's an example of how not to run a bookshop.'

'I think you're forgetting yourself,' Raphael observed, calmly.

Jemma opened her mouth to reply, then pulled her jacket round her and shivered. The weather was ridiculously changeable today. As if in agreement, she heard a rumble. *I was right*, she thought. *There's a storm coming*. And another low, bad-tempered rumble would have confirmed that, if she could have been sure that it came from outside the shop. Something fizzed overhead, followed by a tinkle of broken glass as another lightbulb smashed.

Raphael lifted both hands into the air, as if calming an invisible opponent. 'I suggest you go for a walk, Jemma. I think you need time out of the shop. But before you go, I shall reiterate that I did not send any of those anonymous letters, and I don't know where they came from. You may believe what you like, but that is the truth.' He held her gaze a moment longer, then looked away as if that were the end of the matter.

Jemma was taken aback. She had expected Raphael to mount an indignant defence, at the very least. She had been prepared to counteract any argument he made with damning circumstantial evidence. His refusal to engage irked her. 'Right,' she said. 'Fine. If that's how it is.'

Raphael didn't reply, and didn't look up. So Jemma wrenched the shop door open and slammed it behind her without a backward glance.

She hadn't walked more than a few feet before it started to rain. Not a light drizzle, oh no. Big, fat raindrops that meant business. Jemma pulled up the collar of her jacket and huddled into it, but drops still found their way down her neck, into her pockets, and through her shoulder seams, until she was thoroughly damp. She thought about sheltering in a doorway till the rain had stopped; but the rain didn't look as if it would ever stop. The world was dissolving into a grey mist of rain, losing both colour and definition. The only real thing was Jemma herself: wet, clammy, and indignant.

She had stalked away from the bookshop full of self-righteous purpose. *He'll be lucky if I ever set foot in that shop again.* But the rain, and the accompanying gusts of wind, made striding rather difficult. Jemma's pace slowed even as people scurried past her, holding umbrellas and coats and magazines over their heads. Really, once you were wet through, you couldn't get any wetter, so there wasn't any point in trying to keep dry. Jemma took her hands out of her pockets and turned her face up to the rain. A large cold raindrop splashed into her eye, and she bit back a swearword.

After fifteen minutes of wandering, Jemma wasn't sure where she was, or why. *Raphael*, she thought. *He made a fool of me.* Then she remembered his quiet denial, and frowned. 'But it was him,' she muttered. 'It must have been. Who else would bother?'

She thought about getting her notebook out of her bag, but decided the rain would do it no good. She shivered, and pulled her useless jacket around her.

And now that she had left the shop, of course, there was no rumbling at all. 'Stupid weather,' she muttered, scowling at the rain. It had seemed so very storm-like with the rumbling, and the electricity in the air, and the lights blowing.

'It must have been a storm,' she said aloud. 'There isn't anything else it could be.' Nothing rumbled like that. Unless it had been a tube train going under the shop. But firstly, she was fairly sure that no tube line was near enough, and secondly, she had never heard a rumble like that in all the time she had spent at Burns Books.

Jemma's pace quickened until she was the one scurrying past other pedestrians. She couldn't say why, but she wanted to put as much distance between herself and the shop, and Raphael, as she could. She wanted to be doing normal things, not hurrying through the streets of London in the pouring rain, or dealing with customers' strange requests and finding that yes, actually, they did happen to have that unusual book in stock, or opening boxes of books which seemed determined to tell her something—

'What's the most normal thing I can think of?' she muttered as she sped along, cheeks flushed, arms pumping. 'Who is the most normal person I know?'

A bus shelter reared up at her through the rain, and she flung her hands out to ward it off. 'Watch where you're going, love!' a voice said, and laughed.

Jemma took a step back, and looked. The bus shelter had a huge poster advertising ice cream, of all the ridiculous, inappropriate things on a day like today. Magnum ice cream, with a big gold *M*.

Em.

Of course! Jemma ducked into the bus shelter and rang

Em's mobile. She hoped that she wasn't in a meeting.

The phone rang five times. Jemma sighed out her disappointment, and her warm breath added to the mist.

'Hello, Jemma!' Em sang out. 'You missed a good night last night. There was karaoke and everything.'

'Oh,' said Jemma. Her teeth began to chatter, and she clamped her jaw shut.

'I can't talk for long,' said Em. 'I have to go into a meeting in ten minutes, and I haven't read the stuff yet.' She laughed. 'Same old, same old.' Then a pause. 'Are you all right? You're very quiet.'

'I don't know,' said Jemma. 'I'm soaking wet.'

'Oh dear,' said Em, in the casual manner of someone who has never been absolutely soaked through. 'Did you get caught in the rain?'

'I'm out in it now,' said Jemma. 'My boss told me to go for a walk.'

'In this?' said Em. 'Oh, actually it's stopped raining over here.' Another pause. 'So did you ring me up to tell me that you're soaking wet?'

'I should have listened to you, Em,' said Jemma. 'I tried my best, I really did, and for nothing.' She stared at the rain lashing down all around her.

'Oh,' said Em. 'Is this about that bookshop?'

'Yes,' said Jemma. 'It is. I could have made a success of it, but he wouldn't let me. And now this.'

'Oh dear,' said Em. 'That doesn't sound good. Look, I have to do work stuff, but I'll be thinking about you. In a way I'm glad that it's happened now, and you didn't get hurt worse later on. Men, eh?'

'Yeah,' said Jemma. For no particular reason she thought of Carl the barista, whom she might never see again.

'You can do better than that smelly little bookshop,' said Em, in an encouraging tone. 'I know you can. You just need the right opportunity. When I get out of this meeting I'll ask if anyone knows of an opening. That idiot in the bookshop is taking advantage of you, and I'm glad that you've seen through it. Honestly, Jemma, you'll look back at this in a year's time and laugh. You really will. I have to go, but I'll call you later if I can. Bye, Jemma, bye.' And the call ended.

Jemma gazed at the phone, then put it in her bag. *I knew Em would agree with me.* She imagined herself, nice and dry, returning to the shop to tell Raphael that she had got herself a lovely shiny new job that paid twice what the bookshop did, so he could shove his job where the sun didn't shine. But somehow, as she visualised it, she couldn't see Raphael being angry, or devastated, or even slightly upset. He just listened, and said that that was a shame. She sighed a huge sigh, and pushed sopping rat's-tails of hair away from her face.

It would be nice, though, to go and tell Raphael exactly what she thought of him.

And then she remembered reading in the armchair, and writing the shop's phone number on the customers' bags, and tickling Folio under his chin, and polishing the shop counter, and the tingly feeling she had when she opened a box of books with no idea what she might find inside.

Jemma swallowed, and felt something warm trickle

down her cheek. Absentmindedly, she rubbed it away.

I should listen to Em. Em is sensible. Em knows what's what. Em has a boyfriend, and they have a lovely flat together, and a mortgage, and she doesn't get hangovers. And I could get another job, I know I could.

She stared at the rain. Perhaps she was getting used to it, or perhaps it was a little less misty and blurred than before.

'I can get another job,' she said, and the other ten people in the bus shelter looked at her, then shuffled further off. 'But I don't want to. I want to find out what's going on.'

She peered at the map on the inside of the bus shelter. Somehow, in her wandering, she had managed to travel almost in a complete circle. She was about two minutes' walk from the bookshop. She sighed and stepped out into the rain, which slowed to a drizzle, then stopped entirely.

Chapter 16

Jemma had rehearsed a short, pithy speech in the time it took her to walk back to the bookshop, but the words fled when she pushed open the door. The shop was dark; only one light was on. She wasn't sure whether Raphael had switched the others off, or they had blown. Raphael himself was shelving books, his back to her. It looked as if a bunch of unruly customers had come in and wrecked the place. Books lay randomly on the floor, everything in the window display had been knocked over, and somehow the paper bags had come off the string, and lay around the counter like fallen leaves.

'What happened?' she asked, stepping in carefully.

Raphael turned round, and Jemma braced herself to be shouted at, or worse, disapproved of. 'Oh, it's you,' he said. He didn't look annoyed, or disapproving. But he did look very, very tired. Her heart went out to him, and at the same time her anger dissolved.

'Shall I make tea?' she asked.

Raphael considered her question. 'That would be nice, but best not,' he said. 'I've put Folio in the back room.' As he slid another book onto the shelf Jemma noticed he had a large plaster on his right hand.

'Oh dear,' she said. 'That isn't like Folio.'

'It isn't, usually,' said Raphael, shelving another book. 'I mean, he does occasionally go for a customer or two, when they're being troublesome, but that's different.' He moved along the shelf, bending every so often to pick up more books and replace them. 'That's why I sent you for a walk. I was a bit worried about what might happen if you stayed.'

'I'm sorry I shouted at you and – said what I did,' Jemma said, all in a rush.

'I thought that was the problem, you see,' said Raphael, almost as if she hadn't spoken. 'I thought you were causing the disturbance. But it wasn't just you. It was me, too.'

Jemma opened her mouth, but could think of nothing to say, so she closed it again.

'I thought that once you'd left the shop everything would go back to normal.' Raphael peered at a book, then lifted his long arm and fitted it on a shelf above his head. 'Or what passes for normal, in here. I told myself that without you the shop would calm down. But it got worse. As you can see.' He glanced at Jemma. 'Do you know that you're soaking wet?' he asked.

'It had come to my attention,' said Jemma.

'Well, you can't stay here like that, you'll catch a cold.

Wait there.' He put down his pile of books and strode to the door which led to his rooms upstairs. Two minutes later he was back, with a pair of blue and white striped flannel pyjamas and a purple silk dressing gown.

A despairing feline wail sounded from the back room.

'Are you going to behave yourself, Folio?' Raphael demanded.

There was a pause, then a conciliatory meow.

'Good,' said Raphael. He opened the door and Folio sauntered out, tail flicking. He walked over to Jemma and gazed up at her, his eyes brilliant golden spheres. Jemma stretched out a timid hand, and he rubbed it with his cheek. She heard a gentle sigh. When she looked up, Raphael was watching her.

'I'll go and get changed,' she said, and hurried to the toilet. The pyjamas were, of course, far too long for her, and both the trousers and the sleeves had to be rolled up, but at least she was warm. And the silk dressing gown made her feel rather exotic. She dried her hair with the hand towel, and draped her soaked garments over the radiators in the back of the shop. Then she put the kettle on. If there was ever a time for a large pot of tea, it was now.

'We should probably close the shop,' she called. 'I'm not sure I ought to serve customers wearing your pyjamas.'

Raphael appeared in the doorway. 'I closed it when you left,' he said. 'I couldn't have the customers coming to any harm. After all, it isn't their fault.'

Jemma gave him a curious look. 'What isn't their fault?'

Raphael appeared to be searching for the right word. 'The . . . *atmosphere*.'

The kettle boiled, and Jemma warmed the pot. 'I don't understand anything,' she said. 'I don't understand why someone's sending anonymous letters. I don't understand why you don't want the shop to do well. And I really don't understand why things – things *happen* in here.'

Raphael sighed. 'I'm not sure I can answer all of those questions,' he said. 'But I presume that whoever is sending the anonymous letters wants me, and Burns Books, to disappear. They're trying to frighten us away.' He managed a thin smile. 'It won't happen, but that's what they want.'

Jemma eyed the copy of the *Bookseller's Companion* which was still lying on the counter where she had thrown it. 'They wanted me to think you were sending them, so that I'd leave too.' She frowned. 'But do they want us to leave, or do they want to get hold of the shop? The estate agent said it wasn't worth much.'

'Oh, the estate agent,' Raphael said, with scorn. 'They'll tell you anything.' Then he gave her a quizzical glance. 'Why were you talking to an estate agent about the shop?'

'I wasn't!' exclaimed Jemma. 'Well, I was, but I didn't start it. I was looking in the window when I left the other day, and someone came outside to entice me in, and I said I worked here, and he began talking about the shop. I was thinking of looking at flats, but he kept saying that the area was expensive and dangerous.'

'I see,' said Raphael, grimly.

'Do you think they're involved?' asked Jemma.

Raphael considered. 'To be completely honest, I've no idea how much the shop is worth. For all I know flats round here are expensive. But it seems a bit odd, given the letters.'

Jemma made the tea and fitted the Space Invaders tea cosy over the pot. 'Maybe it's them; maybe it's a rival bookshop owner.' She sighed. 'But let's leave that one aside for now,' she said. 'Why don't you want the shop to do well? I mean, I haven't changed much since I started working here, apart from doing a couple of window displays and talking to the customers, and it's so obvious that with a little bit of love and care, the shop could do really well. Yet the reviews on TripAdvisor are terrible.'

'Love and care isn't the issue,' said Raphael, sounding ruffled.

Jemma got the best cups and saucers out of the cupboard. The occasion seemed to demand it. Then she faced him. 'So what is?' she asked, as gently as she could.

Raphael looked extremely uncomfortable. 'I do care about the shop,' he said. 'Of course I do. It's been in my family for years and years.'

'Yes, I know,' said Jemma. 'You told me. But if you care about the shop, then why is it so tired and shabby?'

'Careful,' warned Raphael.

Jemma looked around nervously, half expecting one of the wall cupboards to fall on her, or at least to be showered with crockery, but apart from a slight momentary heaviness in the air, nothing happened. She lifted down the biscuit barrel and put the last of the custard creams on a plate.

'Don't you start,' muttered Raphael. Jemma glanced at him, surprised, then realised that he wasn't talking to her. 'All right. I haven't done all the things I could for the shop because I need to protect it. I don't want busloads of tourists taking pictures of it, and tagging it on Facebook, and journalists writing it up as a top London destination. The more interest the bookshop gets, the more likely it is that people will ask questions. And I don't want that.'

Jemma poured tea into the cups, thinking all the while. 'A few days ago,' she said, 'you talked about balance, and the shop's niche, and you said that when I'd worked here longer, then I would understand.'

Raphael darted a look at her. 'I did, didn't I?'

Jemma took a deep breath. 'When you said that, I thought you were using it as an excuse for being lazy. I found it frustrating. I wanted to do things to improve the shop, and you wouldn't let me. It was like pushing against a brick wall. When Nafisa gave me the *Bookseller's Companion* I wanted to believe that you had sent the letters, because that made everything your fault. So I jumped to the wrong conclusion. And I'm really sorry.'

Raphael cleared his throat noisily. 'Thank you for your apology. Now shall we get on and drink this tea?'

'I've only worked here a few more days since then,' said Jemma, 'and I don't understand the shop yet. But I'm beginning to, if that makes sense. I think we can make changes in the shop, very gradually, and still maintain a balance. And I think the shop would appreciate that.' She squeezed her eyes shut and braced herself for some sort of catastrophe.

After a few seconds, nothing had happened. Then she heard a chuckle, and felt a vibration on her left ankle. She looked down to find Folio's chubby body pressed against her leg.

'I think you're right,' said Raphael quietly. 'Perhaps the shop has been attracting the wrong sort of attention all this time, and I never realised. I was so busy making sure it didn't become successful that I went too far the other way.'

'But that isn't everything,' said Jemma. 'We have to find out who is sending the letters, and why. And then we have to stop them.'

She waited for a sign. But the cupboard stayed on the wall, Folio continued to purr, and the books remained on the shelves.

'I agree,' said Raphael. 'We have to stop them.' And the sun broke through the clouds outside, and made the shop bright again.

Chapter 17

They basked in the pleasant warmth of the shop, until Raphael spoilt it by asking 'But how?'

'I don't know,' said Jemma. 'We need answers, but I'm not entirely sure what the questions are.' She bit into a biscuit reflectively.

Ping!

'Was that an answer?' asked Raphael with a smile.

'Unfortunately, it was a text message,' said Jemma. She walked over to the coat stand, unhooked her bag, and delved inside for her phone. 'Oh.'

The message was from Em. *Can't talk right now but friend of a friend sent me this. Analyst job, Highgate. Going on job websites next week, but you can get in early.*

Jemma clicked the attachment. The job was at a company she'd heard of, paid roughly what she had earned before, and was well within her capabilities.

'Is it good news?' asked Raphael.

It took Jemma a while to look up from her phone. 'I'm not sure,' she said. She thought about closing the message and telling him that it was just a normal text. But that didn't feel right. 'It's from a friend. She's sent me details of a job in Highgate.'

'That's quite a long way away,' said Raphael.

'Yes, it is,' said Jemma. 'It would be a long commute.' *And a long way from here*, she thought. *In more ways than one.*

'Is it a good job?' asked Raphael. 'I mean, obviously I'd like you to continue working in the shop, but I can't stand in your way.' The words were conventional enough, but Raphael appeared genuinely crestfallen.

'It is a good job,' she said. 'But I didn't ask her to go job-hunting for me.' She pressed *Reply*, and texted *Thanks, I'll have a look X*. 'More tea? I think we can get another cup each out of the pot.'

Jemma was mid-pour when her phone rang. She set the teapot down carefully. 'Em must have finished her meeting,' she said, and pressed *Accept*.

'What do you mean, you'll have a look?' Em demanded. 'I thought you were desperate for another job, after the way that man treated you!'

'Um, hello Em,' said Jemma. 'Thank you for sending me the job, I appreciate it.'

'But you won't follow it up, will you?' said Em. 'In fact, I bet you're in that shop right now. You've gone crawling back, after everything I said. Why do you have to be so stubborn, Jemma? Why won't you listen to me? I'm only trying to do the best for you, believe me. You ought to thank me, and instead you disregard me completely. Well, that's it. That's the last time I help you. I'm through. You're on your own.' She paused, but Jemma felt too battered by her words to venture a reply. 'Goodbye, Jemma.' *Click*.

'Do you need to sit down?' asked Raphael. Jemma nodded, and allowed him to lead her to the armchair and plump up the cushion.

'I don't understand,' she said. 'I suppose that's another one for the list. Sorry. I feel very stupid today.'

'Oh, I wouldn't worry about that,' said Raphael. 'In fact, often it's when we are at our most stupid that we are on the brink of understanding.'

'I hope you're right,' said Jemma. 'Could you pass me my tea?' Raphael obliged, and she sipped thoughtfully. 'She sounded really angry,' she said, in a puzzled tone. 'That's so unlike Em. She's never liked the idea of me working here, though. I remember when I told her I'd got this job. Almost immediately she sent me an article about the worst bookshops, and we were number two.'

'At least we weren't number one,' said Raphael, with a wry smile. 'Who was, if you don't mind me asking?'

'Can't remember,' said Jemma. 'Hang on a minute, I'll look.' She opened her messages, then scrolled up Em's feed. 'Here we are.' But when she clicked on the article, the worst bookshop in Britain wasn't the thing that caught her eye. 'The *Bookseller's Companion*!'

'Yes, it's over there on the counter,' said Raphael.

'No, this is taken from the *Bookseller's Companion*!'

cried Jemma. 'Or at least, the information is.'

'That could be a coincidence, though,' said Raphael.

'It could,' said Jemma. 'But that means Em knows about it. And why is she so keen for me not to work in this particular bookshop? She must know something.' She frowned as she recalled Em's attempt to get her out to the pub the evening before. 'She's been trying to convince me that I'm doing the wrong thing working here. She tried to get me to go drinking with her yesterday, and I didn't because I was going to – do things.' She grimaced as she remembered her hangover. 'She probably wanted to pump me for information. And today another letter came! For me this time, telling me to keep my nose out. And they used – *she* used the *Bookseller's Companion* so I'd think it was you! Or another bookseller, at least. But I bet she wanted to pin it on you.'

'But how would she know you were looking into the letters?' said Raphael. 'Had you told her about it?'

'No, I haven't said a word. But I got home late yesterday partly because I popped into the estate agent. The moment I mentioned the shop, he started telling me that it wasn't worth anything and I shouldn't move into the area.'

'I could be wrong,' said Raphael, 'but it sounds as if she's warning you off.'

'You're right,' said Jemma. 'From what, though? What's going to happen?'

Raphael shrugged. 'Search me. Your friend isn't an estate agent, is she?'

'Oh gosh, no,' said Jemma. 'She was a colleague of

126

mine until two weeks ago.' Then she gasped. 'But her boyfriend is. And the day I left work she wasn't there, because she had a day off. They were celebrating Damon's new job.'

'Hmm,' said Raphael. 'This sounds suspicious. I don't suppose you know which estate agency he's with?'

'No idea,' said Jemma. 'But I bet I can find out.' She opened Google and typed *Damon Foskett estate agent.*

A page of results came up, and images of Damon smiling in black tie at various industry bashes. In one he was even clutching an award. But the one that caught Jemma's eye was an announcement from Ransome's. 'We are delighted to welcome Damon Foskett as Commercial Manager of our two Westminster branches.' She showed Raphael. 'That's good enough for me,' she said grimly. 'I imagine that if you'd gone into the branch and asked for a valuation, they'd have spun you the same tale as they did me: that the shop wasn't worth a great deal.'

'I'd expect nothing less from an estate agent,' said Raphael. 'But while you think your friend sent the letter to warn you off, the letters to me were designed to make me sell up and leave.' He mused for a moment. 'This Damon, would you say he is a particularly evil chap?'

'Not particularly,' said Jemma. 'Very focused on his job, but so am I.'

'Do you know,' said Raphael, 'I might recognise that young man. Can you show me the pictures again?'

Jemma passed Raphael her phone. She noted that he knew how to enlarge the images with his thumb and forefinger. *He knows more about technology than he lets on.*

Raphael held the phone at arm's-length, and looked over his glasses at it. 'Yes, I'm almost sure,' he said. 'Obviously he's a lot smarter there, but I had an assistant called Dave, for a short time, and I'm sure that's him.'

'Really?' said Jemma. 'When was this?'

'Oh, maybe a year ago,' said Raphael. 'He was a funny one, Dave. I mean, funnier than most of my assistants. Very keen on his first day, then kept disappearing into the stockroom. By Wednesday, I had to fetch him out of there at the end of the day. Then he disappeared completely. Never saw him again. I couldn't work out if he'd left of his own accord, or if the shop had been up to mischief. But as no one came asking, I thought least said, soonest mended.' He examined the photo. 'Yes, Dave had big black-rimmed glasses, and stubble, and he normally wore a baseball cap, but I'm pretty sure that's him.'

'He must have been looking for something,' said Jemma. 'I wonder what it was? And did he find it?'

'You could interpret the situation two ways,' said Raphael. 'Either he did find it, but couldn't get it out of the shop, or else he didn't find it but he knows it's here, and he wants to keep searching.' His fists clenched. 'I was rather sorry when Dave disappeared, but now I wish that the shop had done its worst.'

'What do you think he's looking for?' said Jemma.

'If he's an estate agent, I assume he wants money,' said Raphael.

Jemma gave him a significant look. 'Raphael, would you mind answering a question?'

Raphael looked deeply guilty. 'It depends what it is,' he said.

'Do you know of anything about the shop which would make an estate agent keen to get hold of it?'

Raphael's expression lightened immediately. 'Not in the slightest,' he said. 'Several windows need repairing, the bathroom upstairs is cramped, and the central heating is temperamental. Not to mention the decor.'

'Hmm,' said Jemma. 'Bear with me a moment.' She unlocked her phone, made use of Google, and typed in a phone number. 'This might not work,' she said, 'but I found the number for Westminster Council's planning department. Can you ask them about any enquiries for this address?'

'I'll give it a try,' said Raphael. He pressed the dial button, and when someone answered, slipped into a near-perfect imitation of Damon's voice. 'Hello? Just calling to follow up 139A Charing Cross Road? Yeah, I'll hold.' He covered the mouthpiece and grinned at Jemma, who was gaping at him. 'Yeah, yeah, still here. Oh yeah, haha, fab. Right then. Yeah, that's cool. Bye.'

He ended the call. 'The cheeky monkey!' he exclaimed. 'The council official kindly informed me that they would welcome a change of use for this premises from a bookshop to a wine bar, provided that the proposed alterations were made.'

'*What?*' said Jemma.

'I haven't finished,' said Raphael. 'She also said that no, I wouldn't need planning permission to carry out works in an existing basement.' Then he frowned. 'But the shop doesn't have a basement.'

'Damon thinks it does,' said Jemma. 'And Damon appears to have plans for the shop.' She reached for a custard cream and snapped it in two. 'I think we should put Damon straight, don't you?'

Chapter 18

The next day, Raphael opened up the shop and they carried on in the usual way. Customers came, they sold them books and made a reasonable profit, and everyone was happy.

Everyone, that is, except Raphael. 'Can't we just get this over with?' he grumbled, almost before one customer had left the shop.

'Not yet,' said Jemma. 'We have to be patient. We have to wait for them to make the next move.' She opened up her phone and read Em's message again. 'Em said this job will be advertised next week, and today's Thursday. I don't think they'll leave it much longer.' She smiled. 'Why don't you take a nice long lunch break?'

Raphael glanced around furtively. 'Do you think they'll suspect anything if I do that?'

'I doubt it,' said Jemma, laughing. She went to fetch

more books from the stockroom, and when she opened the box, found it full of John le Carré novels. 'There,' she said, holding up *Tinker Tailor Soldier Spy*. 'That settles it.'

Raphael rubbed his hands. 'Much as I dislike the idea of acting on the questionable messages of a random selection of books, on this occasion I'll humour you.'

Jemma stared at him. 'Do you mean to say that your actions are based on logic and reasoning?'

'Now I never said that,' said Raphael, and left before she could question him further.

Jemma tried her best not to watch the door. She shelved books, she went into the back room and made tea, she even popped into the stockroom. But nothing happened. She was beginning to despair when two men wearing deerstalkers, claiming to be from the Baker Street Irregulars, came in looking for what they described as Sherlockiana. Jemma was kept busy pulling out monographs about cigar ash, suggested chronologies of the stories, and theories of what Dr Watson had really done in the war. When they left, grasping two dusty volumes each, she was gratified to see that her patience had paid off. There, on the mat, lay a long white envelope.

Jemma hurried over and picked it up. It was addressed in wobbly capitals as if the person had been in a hurry. Or disguising their handwriting. Her thumb moved instinctively to the flap, then stopped. *I'll wait. We should open it together.*

She didn't have long to wait. Raphael came in, looked enquiringly at her, then exclaimed as Jemma pointed to the counter, where the envelope lay neatly squared up.

132

'It worked!' he cried. 'I knew it!'

Jemma cleared her throat noisily. 'Shall we open it?' she asked.

Raphael glanced at her, and she saw a mischievous spark in his blue eyes. 'Yes,' he said, smiling. 'Let's.' And he picked the envelope up, and handed it to her.

Jemma ripped the envelope open and withdrew the letter. It was on white A4 paper again, folded into thirds. She unfolded it, laid it on the counter, then came round to Raphael's side.

gAMe's Up. WE've gOT pRooF. BeSt QuiT wHiLe You'Re aHEaD

Raphael recoiled from the letter and put a hand to his brow. 'Oh no!' he cried. 'I am ruined!'

Jemma stared at him. 'What are you talking about?'

Raphael clutched at his sandy hair, then put his face in his hands. 'I'm putting on a show in case anyone's watching,' he murmured.

'Oh no!' exclaimed Jemma. She put her hands to her mouth, and opened her eyes as wide as she could.

Raphael snatched up the letter and strode off to the back room. 'I shall make tea,' he said, out of the side of his mouth.

'All done,' said Raphael, sauntering into the shop twenty minutes later. 'I've done some very conspicuous packing in my front room, and I have phoned Ransome's and asked for someone to come and do a valuation of the shop. They are coming at two.'

'That's quick,' said Jemma.

'It is rather, isn't it?' said Raphael, his expression deadpan.

'Shall I text Em, then?' Jemma found it hard not to grin as she said this.

'Why not,' said Raphael. 'Actually, pop into the back. You wouldn't want me to know you were a rat leaving the sinking ship, would you?'

'True,' said Jemma, and scurried off. She opened her messages, and texted.

I'm so sorry about yesterday. My emotions were all over the place. Now I've slept on it, you're right. Things here are too unstable. I'll polish my CV when I get in tonight. Thank you for being a true friend, Jemma X

She read it through. In some ways, she thought, the message was true. She was sorry that Em had chosen Damon's nasty plan over their friendship. Her emotions had been all over the place. And things at the shop, it had to be said, were frequently unstable. *But somehow, that's how I like it.* And she pressed *Send*.

They closed the shop at a quarter to two, to give themselves breathing space before things kicked off. Jemma had popped round to the mini-market for a sandwich, but when she unwrapped it, she found herself unable to eat more than a couple of bites.

'Are you all right?' asked Raphael, as she put her unfinished sandwich back into the packaging.

Jemma grimaced. 'A bit nervous, I guess.'

Raphael grinned. 'Haven't you been on a training course to deal with that sort of thing?'

134

Jemma raised her eyebrows. 'What, a training course on managing your emotions when your best friend and her scummy boyfriend are trying to cheat your employer and take away your job?' She laughed.

'You know what I mean,' said Raphael. 'Emotional intelligence, or resilience, or one of those sorts of things.'

Jemma stared at him. 'How do you know about those sorts of things? I didn't think you paid attention to management jargon.'

'I don't,' said Raphael. 'But as a business owner, I know all about resilience.'

Folio, who had been mysteriously absent for most of the morning, made his entrance with a bloodcurdling yowl, then leapt onto the counter and followed up with a purr.

'Don't peak too early, Folio,' said Raphael, rubbing his cheek. 'You must have your company manners ready for the nice man.'

'Have I seen Folio's company manners?' asked Jemma.

'Let's hope you don't,' said Raphael darkly.

At one minute past two they heard three sharp knocks at the door. 'Here we go,' said Raphael. Jemma retreated to the fiction shelves and picked up a pile of books she had left there, and Raphael opened the door.

In walked Damon, in a new-looking navy suit. 'Good afternoon, Mr . . . Burns, is it?'

'That's right,' said Raphael, pumping Damon's hand up and down till Damon winced. 'I take it you're the estate agent.'

'Yes. Commercial manager, actually. Damon Foskett, at your service.' Raphael released his hand and Damon flexed it for a moment, then massaged it gently.

'Excellent. I am Raphael Burns, and this is my assistant Jemma.'

Damon followed Raphael's gaze, and a slow smile spread over his face. 'Well, well! I didn't know you worked here! I mean, Em said something about you having a new job, and I think she mentioned books…'

Jemma nodded. She didn't trust herself to speak.

'So, shall we get on?' asked Raphael, rubbing his hands.

'By all means,' said Damon. He pulled out a laser measuring device and started pointing it at the walls of the shop. 'Hmm.' He took out a notebook and pen, and scribbled numbers. 'Mind if I go into the back?'

'Be my guest,' said Raphael. He followed Damon and Jemma waited, her heart in her mouth.

They returned a few minutes later, and Damon looked glum. 'I'm afraid it isn't brilliant news, Mr Burns.'

'Oh, but don't you want to see upstairs?' asked Raphael.

'I'm assuming it's the usual over-the-shop kind of thing,' said Damon. 'Bedroom, living room, small kitchen, small bathroom, box room? Maybe a balcony, if you're lucky.'

Raphael nodded, the corners of his mouth turned down.

'Then I don't need to see it,' said Damon, and snapped his notebook shut. 'It isn't a great time to sell, truth be told. Very slow at this time of year. Obviously I'll give you the best price I can, because I know your delightful assistant.' He winked at Jemma, who managed a smile in return. 'So this is what I think it's worth. And that's at the

136

top end, mind.' He opened his notebook again, scribbled a number, and showed it to them both.

Raphael whistled. 'Gosh, that's rather low.'

'That's the market at the moment, you see,' said Damon, with a sigh.

'Oh, I'm sure it is,' said Raphael. 'But I was hoping for more. The other estate agents' valuations were higher than yours.'

'Other estate agents?' said Damon, frowning.

'They do exist,' said Raphael. 'I thought it best to get a few quotes, you see. Sound business practice, and all that.'

Jemma hid a smile. It had been her idea to book two valuations the evening before, when she judged that Damon would probably be at home with Em, a pile of newspapers, and a pot of glue.

'Oh, I see,' said Damon. 'They were probably trying to reel you in, mind. Some of the less scrupulous estate agencies do that. They get you on their books, then once the place has failed to sell they drop the price to exactly my figure. If you want a quick sale, we're the company to go with.'

Raphael looked thoughtful. 'I do see your point,' he said. 'And I am interested in a quick sale. You see, my assistant and I have been subject to a hate campaign recently. Anonymous letters.'

Damon assumed a concerned expression. 'Oh dear,' he said. 'I am sorry to hear that.'

'Don't worry,' said Raphael. 'It's in the hands of the police. We got another letter this morning, if you can believe that. Actually, Jemma, would you mind taking it round to the station? The detective inspector did say we ought to submit any further evidence promptly.'

'I'm sure that can wait until I've finished,' said Damon. A hopeful, slightly nervous smile appeared on his face. 'Actually, could I take another peek at the back premises? I don't think I appreciated the full extent of the stockroom.'

'I don't know what you mean,' said Raphael. 'I thought you took measurements.'

'Oh yes, so I did,' said Damon. 'Perhaps I was a little hasty in my calculations. Let me look again.' He opened his notebook, and inspected the page. 'I could push the valuation maybe fifty thousand higher.'

'That's promising,' said Raphael, 'but I don't think it's enough. After all, if you're planning to make this place into a wine bar, I'm sure you'll get a much better return on it.'

Damon stared at him. 'A – a wine bar?' he faltered.

'Yes, a wine bar,' said Jemma. 'I suggested we check in with the planning department at the council. Strangely, they thought Raphael was a Mr Foskett, who had enquired about this very premises, the possibility of turning it into a wine bar, and doing work on the basement.'

Damon ran a hand round the back of his collar. 'Very common name, Foskett. And London's a big place.'

'That it is,' said Raphael. 'I suppose I ought to thank you for uncovering something I never knew about my own shop.'

Damon opened his mouth to speak, but Raphael held up a hand. 'Jemma is an expert in finding things out. We were puzzled because, as far as we knew, the shop didn't have a basement. But after a bit of Googling, and investigation of lost buildings of London, and plenty of staring at maps and plans, we found evidence. I imagine you know what I'm referring to.'

Damon swallowed again. 'Yes,' he squeaked.

'I thought you would,' said Raphael. 'When you worked here briefly as my assistant, you spent an awful lot of time in that stockroom. I did wonder if it would eat you alive at one point.'

Damon tried to look innocent. 'Assistant? What do you mean?'

'You know exactly what he means, *Dave*,' said Jemma, and Damon had the grace to blush.

'All right,' he said, 'so I have a particular interest in this property. An affection for it, even. What's wrong with that? It's normal for an estate agent to have an interest in property. That's why we do the job.' He sighed. 'How about a joint venture, Mr Burns? I'll make you a handsome offer for half the property, I'll get our team to develop it, and fit out the basement, and get it set up as a wine bar, and we'll split the profits. You won't have to do a day's work ever again.'

Raphael's brow furrowed. 'Half the profits, you say? What would you estimate that at, per annum?'

Damon turned to a new page in his notebook. 'Well, I'd say the fit-out will cost about *this*, and obviously that's an upfront cost which I'd want to recoup from the business, but I would estimate that once that's paid off, you could be looking at this much.' He scribbled a figure, and held it up.

'Mmm,' said Raphael, with a gleam in his eye. 'That *is*

139

interesting. And I'd never have to do a day's work again, you say?'

Jemma's jaw dropped. Damon the slime-ball had found Raphael's weak spot, and she had a horrible feeling that he had won. She eyed his smug smile, and her heart plummeted into her baseball boots.

Chapter 19

'No!' cried Jemma. 'Raphael, you can't! What about the history of the shop? What about the customers? What will they do if we're not here?'

Raphael shrugged. 'They'll find another bookshop,' he said. 'After all, there are plenty on this road.'

Damon laughed. 'I'm surprised at you, Jemma,' he said. 'What about that business brain? What about that ambition?' He looked at her, and his lip curled. 'Em was right. This shop's done something to you.'

Jemma drew herself up. 'Yes, it has,' she said, her eyes flashing fire. 'It's given me something to aim for besides success. It's given me a purpose. It's given me satisfaction. And it makes people happy. If that's wrong, then *I'm* wrong, and I don't care.' She felt tears prickling at the back of her eyes, and fled to the bathroom. *I'm not going to cry in front of Damon Foskett*, she thought, as she washed her face in cold water and scrubbed it dry with the scratchy towel. Whatever else he told Em when they were celebrating their success tonight, he couldn't tell her that.

Raphael cleared his throat. 'So, this mysterious basement. We've looked at plans and maps and whatnot, and we're sure it's there, but we haven't actually found a way into it yet. Have you had any luck, Mr Foskett?'

Jemma emerged from the bathroom, dry-eyed and shamefaced. She couldn't run away. She had to see how things played out, however bad it was. And she was most definitely a spectator, as the men stood close together.

The corner of Damon's mouth turned up in a slow, cunning smile. 'It's not easy to find, Mr Burns. As you now know, I tried when I worked here, and I had no luck. But after a bit more investigation on the internet, I'm pretty sure I can uncover it now. Come this way.' And he opened the door of the stockroom, and invited Raphael in. Jemma followed, her heart in her mouth.

Damon switched on the lights, pulled out his phone, and opened an app. 'Compass,' he said, in explanation. 'Now if I'm right, it's ten steps north, five steps east.' He began to pace. 'Course, I might not be exactly spot on. Depends how long a pace is, doesn't it?' He took ten steps down one of the aisles and stopped at a break in the shelving. 'That's convenient,' he said, in a pleased tone, and turned right, counting under his breath. 'Should be about here,' he said, pointing to his feet. 'Any chance we can get this carpeting rolled back?'

'I should think so,' said Raphael, rolling up his sleeves. 'Come on, Jemma.'

Jemma sighed, and followed suit. They rolled up the carpet, and the underlay, and some ancient, stiff linoleum, until they arrived at wooden floorboards and a trapdoor with an iron ring set into it.

'Looks like I was right,' said Damon, smiling.

'It does,' replied Raphael. 'Would you like to open it?'

Damon grasped the iron ring, and pulled. The trapdoor swung open, revealing a flight of stone steps which were worn in the middle.

'Twelfth century, they say,' breathed Damon. 'The crypt of a lost cathedral. It'll be the talk of London.' He switched on the torch app on his phone. 'Mind if I…? I mean, it's your shop, but it might not be safe, and I'm insured for this sort of thing.'

'Oh no, absolutely,' said Raphael. 'Please, go ahead.'

Damon didn't need telling twice. A second later he was heading down the steps. He disappeared, then the light from his torch faded too.

Raphael nudged Jemma and gave her an enormous wink.

'Woah,' Damon exclaimed, and the cellar echoed it. 'This is amazing.'

Jemma clutched Raphael's arm, and strained her ears to hear more. There was nothing for a few seconds, then a muttered 'Hang on a minute—'

The next sound was a rush of water. A shriek followed, then the whoosh of a giant wave breaking against a wall. 'Help!' cried Damon. Then 'Shit! Pike!' His exclamation was followed by frenzied splashing. Then another cry, followed by 'What the heck? Get off me!' More splashing.

'Since when have there been octopuses in London?'

Jemma looked at Raphael, who was shaking with silent laughter. 'He won't die, will he?' she whispered.

Raphael glanced at her, and shook his head. Folio trotted up, peered into the hole, and gave a small meow.

They heard more splashing, then a murmured 'Thank God for that,' and the sound of feet squelching up the steps. Damon appeared out of the darkness. His hair was plastered to his head, the navy suit, now black, clung to him, and he clutched a dripping phone.

'I take it the cellar requires extensive work, then?' said Raphael, and laughed.

Damon fixed him with a look of pure hatred. 'Get out of my way,' he said.

'Now, now,' said Raphael. 'No need to be rude.' But he didn't step aside. 'Don't ever come back here, Mr Foskett,' he said, quietly. 'And if you know what's good for you, you will go far, far away. Because if you bother me again…' He leaned closer, until he was almost touching Damon's dripping nose. 'There will be consequences.'

Damon swallowed, and nodded. Raphael stepped aside, and the estate agent squidged off, leaving only a trail of water.

'That was rather fun,' said Raphael, closing the trapdoor. 'I propose a cup of tea while you finish your sandwich, and then we can open up the shop.' He kicked the floor coverings into place.

'But – but—' Jemma pointed at the floor. 'None of the documents said the entrance was there!'

'No, they didn't, did they?' said Raphael. 'And I don't

think it is. I think that poor young man imagined it. Look.'
He rolled everything back again, and Jemma stared at the
place where the trapdoor had been, and where the
floorboards were now as solid and uniform as their
neighbours.

Then she stared at Raphael. 'So where is it?'

'Where do you think it is?' he asked.

'The maps and plans say there is a staircase in the back
room,' said Jemma. 'There isn't room, though. It can't be
there.'

'No such word as can't,' said Raphael. 'You'll be telling
me next that there isn't a bloodthirsty octopus living in our
cellar.'

Jemma frowned. 'There isn't, is there?'

Raphael shrugged. 'Might be.'

They went into the back room, and Jemma pointed at
the wall. 'It's supposed to be about two feet past there. But
there's nothing. I even sneaked into the yard the other day,
and there's no sign of any staircase whatsoever.'

'I see,' said Raphael. 'I wonder...' He pointed at the
floor. 'Isn't that his little gadget thingy?'

Jemma switched the laser measure on, moved back to
the doorway, and pointed the little red dot at the wall. Then
she read the display. 'See? Two feet short.'

Raphael advanced to the wall and knocked on it.
'Sounds hollow,' he said. 'If that was an outside wall, it
would be made of brick. Jemma, can you fetch the
sledgehammer? You'll find it under the sink.'

Jemma did as she was told, and Raphael hefted the
sledgehammer. 'Stand clear, please. Apart from anything

else, if I'm wrong then the whole shop might collapse.' He drew his arms back, and swung.

Plaster and wood splintered, and stale air rushed out. Jemma switched her phone into torch mode, and shone it through the hole. 'I can see steps!' she said. 'Keep swinging, Raphael, keep swinging.'

Raphael obliged, until there was a hole big enough to step through. Then he turned to Jemma. 'Do you want to go first, or shall I?'

'We'll go together,' said Jemma.

Carefully they stepped into the space, and Jemma illuminated the stairs with her phone. The steps, oddly, looked less worn than the ones Damon had descended. She made to take a step, then paused. 'There won't be a killer octopus down there, will there? Or an underground river?'

'I can't promise anything,' said Raphael. 'But I doubt it. Let's go and see.'

The staircase was wide enough for them to walk side by side, and handholds had been left in the brickwork. Their footsteps were quiet on the stone. Jemma listened for water, but heard nothing.

The steps went down a long way. As they descended, a large wooden door with iron hinges came into view. Jemma clutched Raphael's arm. 'It's your shop,' she said. 'You should open it.' She glanced up at him, and he looked as nervous as she felt.

'To think,' he said quietly, 'that my own shop can still surprise me.' He grasped the latch, and lifted it.

The door swung open.

'Woah,' they said, together.

Chapter 20

Jemma looked at her watch as she strolled down Charing Cross Road. She had plenty of time, even though Rolando's didn't open until eight thirty. Or at least, not for most people. She did her special knock on the window, and Carl made a face at her through the glass, then opened the door. 'Usual?' he asked.

'Yes please,' said Jemma.

'Better come in, then,' he said. 'Before you attract the attention of the coffee-drinking zombies.'

'Can't have that.' Jemma grinned, then stepped inside and fished her reusable cup out of her bag.

The coffee machine was already on, and Carl set to work. 'Getting ready for a busy day at the bookshop, then?'

'Something like that,' said Jemma. 'It's window-display day, and we've got someone coming to quote for building work.'

'Extending your evil empire, huh?' Carl set the milk frothing.

'Absolutely,' said Jemma. 'You'll have to come and see when it's finished.'

'I will,' said Carl. 'So long as you don't expect me to make any literary comments.' He sprinkled cocoa powder on the top of her cappuccino. 'That's two pounds seventy-five, with the reusable cup.' Jemma paid with her phone, then handed him her loyalty card. 'And the next one is free,' said Carl, stamping it and handing it back.

'Excellent,' said Jemma. 'Thanks, Carl. See you tomorrow.'

'Yes,' said Carl. He ran a hand over his twists, as if checking they were still there. 'Unless you pop in for lunch? We've got quiche Lorraine on the specials board today.'

Jemma looked regretful, and patted her bag. 'And I've got a homemade pasta salad that I can't cheat on,' she replied. 'Maybe tomorrow.' She took her coffee, and pulled the door to behind her. Two passers-by stopped at the shop, read the *Closed* sign, and murmured in a discontented manner.

Jemma glanced up at the bookshop sign as she approached. It was much clearer now that Raphael had got it repainted. He'd been cagey at first when she asked, worried that she would want him to accept a new design, or worse, call in an agency to present a range of options. Once Jemma had said that the sign was fine, but so faded that nobody could read it, he'd been happy to agree. *Next up, frontage*, thought Jemma. But she was picking her battles at the moment, and she felt that one could wait. After all, she had got her way on Saturday opening.

She fished in her bag for the keys, and opened up the shop. Everything was in order. The counter shone with polishing, the shelves were crammed with books waiting to be read, and the armchair invited customers to sit down and do just that. 'Hello,' she called. 'Morning, Folio.'

Folio walked into the shop, stretched out his right paw in salute, and executed a big stretch. 'No sign of Raphael yet, then,' she said, and Folio purred. 'I'll take that as a no.'

Jemma wandered through to the back room and eyed the large hole in the wall. Raphael had neatened it up a little since they had smashed through a few weeks ago, but its edges were still ragged. He had resisted any further entreaties from Jemma to do something with it, saying that that was what the builders would be paid to do. Once they had decided what the space was for.

'Raphael! I'm just going downstairs,' called Jemma, and climbed carefully through the gap. Folio put his front paws on the bottom edge of the hole, then leapt gracefully through and ran down the stairs ahead of her.

On that first day the cat had lurked at the top of the stairs, looking more apprehensive than Jemma had ever seen him, but Raphael had beckoned him, then scooped him up into his arms and carried him through the door. Folio's eyes grew as wide and dark as saucers as he took it in; the high vaulted ceiling with decorated bosses, the carved stone columns, the sheer size of it all. Jemma had expected to find it scary, or at least creepy, but actually, once she had adjusted her mind to the scale of it, the crypt didn't worry her in the slightest. *It's been here for eight hundred years*, she thought, *and it's survived. Frankly, it's probably in a better state than the rest of the shop.* Folio, once he had explored it thoroughly, seemed to agree with her.

They were still debating what to do with it. Jemma could absolutely see it as a reading area and café, but she didn't want to compete with Rolando's, so she had suggested extending their book stock, perhaps moving the fiction section downstairs, and introducing sofas, armchairs, side tables, and desk lamps. 'It could be a cathedral of reading,' she said.

'Or it could be my basement den,' said Raphael.

Jemma goggled at him. 'A basement den? This? Seriously?'

'Why not?' said Raphael. 'I'd have room for my hobbies then.'

Jemma's eyes narrowed. 'Do you have any hobbies?'

'Not really,' said Raphael. 'I've never had the space, you see. But now...' He rubbed his hands, then caught Jemma's disgusted look and burst out laughing. 'You're far too easy to wind up, Jemma James.'

And that was where they had left it. Jemma hoped that getting a builder round would focus Raphael on the task in hand. Structurally, everything appeared sound to her. And they had already invited over a couple of people from the planning department, who had hummed and hawed over tea in the bookshop, and then, having descended the staircase with them, gasped and raved about the space and the potential.

Of course, whatever Raphael decided to do would require at least some money to fit out. When she had explained that to him, he had sighed as if the world were on his shoulders. But Jemma had, very gently, shown him the daily takings of the bookshop, introduced him to a simple projection of what the shop could reasonably expect to earn in a month, then set that against the figures she had coaxed out of him for the utility bills, Folio's food, and her wages (now a slightly larger sum than before). 'So the shop is making a profit,' she said. 'But if we could get that number higher...' She pointed at the income line. 'Then our profit would be higher too, and we could get the shop sorted more quickly. Once we do that, we'll have much more space for customers. We could even put another till in downstairs.'

'I'm not sure I like the sound of that,' said Raphael. 'That would mean we'd have to be on different floors all the time. I wouldn't be able to go out and – see to things.'

'Maybe,' said Jemma. 'Or we could hire another assistant, perhaps.' She had wondered briefly whether she could tempt Carl away from Rolando's, then realised that might mean no more early cappuccinos. But that was a discussion for the future.

Jemma picked up the camping lantern they'd left at the top of the stairs, switched it on, descended carefully, and opened the great door for Folio, who thanked her with a sharp meow. She drank her cappuccino gazing around the vast, shadowy space, then put her arms out and spun round

151

and round until she was lightheaded. *We could hold events. Book readings, or even theatre.* She imagined rows and rows of chairs, and a rapt audience gazing at Hamlet declaiming to a skull.

A cough almost made Jemma fall over her own feet. She came to a stop just in time and frowned at Raphael, who was leaning on the door frame and smiling at her. 'Getting a feel for the space, are we?'

'Before I was interrupted, yes,' said Jemma. 'We could have events down here.'

Raphael ambled in and gazed around him. 'We could, yes. We could do all sorts of things. Not a wine bar, though,' he added hastily. 'I don't think Rolando would be too happy about that.' He eyed Jemma's cup. 'Is that another cappucino?'

'Maybe,' said Jemma. 'Speaking of not too happy, did you ever go into the estate agent's and tell them what Damon had been up to?'

Raphael shook his head. 'It didn't seem worth it,' he said. 'I don't think Mr Foskett will ever bother us again, and hopefully he's learnt his lesson.' He looked at Jemma. 'Did you hear anything from your friend?'

'Not directly,' said Jemma. 'But I did see a post on her Instagram feed about London being for losers, with a photograph of fields and blue sky. She'd tagged it RuralWins.'

'I see,' said Raphael. He regarded Jemma for a while without speaking. 'Do you miss her?'

Jemma shrugged. 'In a way. She was trying to protect me,' she replied. 'I think I was supposed to be grateful.

But if I'd listened to her I would have walked out of here on my first day, and we'd never have found this, and I'd never have learned the things I have.'

Raphael gave her a pained glance. 'I do hope you haven't been at the management literature again, Jemma.'

'Will you be quiet?' said Jemma, and grinned. 'Why don't you accept the compliment, and put the kettle on. It's half an hour to opening time.'

'Good heavens, is it really?' said Raphael. 'And it's window-display day.'

'It is,' said Jemma, 'but I won't be doing that until twelve o'clock. The regulars get ever so disappointed if I move it.'

'What is it today?' asked Raphael.

'Beach reads,' said Jemma. 'I've got a sandpit, some inflatable beachballs, buckets and spades, several plastic starfish, and a striped windbreaker ready to deploy.'

'Do you think that will work?' said Raphael.

'I don't see why not,' said Jemma. 'Window-display day's always our best sales day. If it doesn't bring people in, I'll change it.'

'I've said it before, and I'll say it again,' said Raphael, bending to stroke Folio. 'People are strange.'

'Whereas this bookshop is perfectly normal, I suppose,' said Jemma.

Raphael chuckled. 'I wouldn't go that far.' He gazed at the dramatic space before him; the arches in sharp relief, the pillars with their lurking shadows. 'It's certainly been an interesting few weeks since you came, Jemma.' He smiled. 'And at least that chump of an estate agent never found out what I was really up to.'

'What do you mean, up to?' demanded Jemma. '*Are* you up to something?'

Raphael straightened his face hastily. 'Who, me? Up to something? Not a sausage. I'm not, am I, Folio?'

Jemma crouched down and looked into the cat's face for a sign, but Folio's amber eyes were as inscrutable as ever.

Acknowledgements

My first thanks go to my super-fast beta readers, who absolutely whipped through this book – Carol Bissett, Ruth Cunliffe, Paula Harmon, and Stephen Lenhardt – and to my excellent proofreader, John Croall. Thank you all for your input and enthusiasm; and yes, there will be a sequel!

A massive additional thank you to my husband Stephen for his continued support. Sorry I didn't murder anyone in this book – maybe next time!

Another big thank you to Audrey Cowie, who gave me the idea for a story set in a bookshop.

And my final thanks go to you, the reader. If you've come to this book having read my historical or cozy mysteries, I hope you enjoyed this slight departure from the norm! I had a brilliant time writing about Jemma, Raphael, Folio and of course the bookshop, and I hope you enjoyed it too. If you did, a short review or rating on

Amazon or Goodreads would be very much appreciated. Ratings and reviews, however short, help readers to discover books.

FONT AND IMAGE CREDITS

Cover and heading fonts: Alyssum Blossom and Alyssum Blossom Sans by Bombastype

Book: Vintage books vector by macrovector_official at freepik.com: https://www.freepik.com/free-vector/books-set-black-white_4352249.htm

Cat (flipped and cropped): Cats silhouettes pack vector by freepik at freepik.com: https://www.freepik.com/free-vector/cats-silhouettes-pack_719787.htm

Letters: taken from Royal Mail pattern free vector by nenilkime at freepik.com: https://www.freepik.com/free-vector/royal-mail-pattern_1380839.htm

Stars: Night free icon by flaticon at freepik.com: https://www.freepik.com/free-icon/night_914336.htm

Chapter vignette: Opened books in hand drawn style Free Vector by freepik at freepik.com: https://www.freepik.com/free-vector/opened-books-hand-drawn-style_765567.htm

Cover created using GIMP image editor: https://www.gimp.org

About the Author

Liz Hedgecock grew up in London, England, did an English degree, and then took forever to start writing. After several years working in the National Health Service, some short stories crept into the world. A few even won prizes. Then the stories started to grow longer…

Now Liz travels between the nineteenth and twenty-first centuries, murdering people. To be fair, she does usually clean up after herself.

Liz's reimaginings of Sherlock Holmes, her Pippa Parker cozy mystery series, the Caster & Fleet Victorian mystery series (written with Paula Harmon), and the Maisie Frobisher Mysteries are available in ebook and paperback.

Liz lives in Cheshire with her husband and two sons, and when she's not writing or child-wrangling you can usually find her reading, messing about on Twitter, or cooing over stuff in museums and art galleries. That's her story, anyway, and she's sticking to it.

Website/blog: http://lizhedgecock.wordpress.com
Facebook: http://www.facebook.com/lizhedgecockwrites
Twitter: http://twitter.com/lizhedgecock
Goodreads: https://www.goodreads.com/lizhedgecock

Books by Liz Hedgecock

Short stories
The Secret Notebook of Sherlock Holmes
Bitesize
The Adventure of the Scarlet Rosebud

Halloween Sherlock series (novelettes)
The Case of the Snow-White Lady
Sherlock Holmes and the Deathly Fog
The Case of the Curious Cabinet

Sherlock & Jack series (novellas)
A Jar Of Thursday
Something Blue
A Phoenix Rises

Mrs Hudson & Sherlock Holmes series (novels)
A House Of Mirrors
In Sherlock's Shadow

Pippa Parker Mysteries (novels)
Murder At The Playgroup
Murder In The Choir
A Fete Worse Than Death
Murder in the Meadow
The QWERTY Murders
Past Tense

Caster & Fleet Mysteries (with Paula Harmon)
The Case of the Black Tulips
The Case of the Runaway Client
The Case of the Deceased Clerk
The Case of the Masquerade Mob
The Case of the Fateful Legacy
The Case of the Crystal Kisses

Maisie Frobisher Mysteries (novels)
All At Sea
Off The Map
Gone To Ground

The Magic Bookshop (short novels)
Every Trick in the Book

For children (with Zoe Harmon)
A Christmas Carrot

WHITE
RHINO
BOOKS

160

Printed in Great Britain
by Amazon